Breaking the Rules

Breaking the Rules

SANDRA GLOVER

Andersen Press · London

First published in 1998 by
Andersen Press Limited,
20 Vauxhall Bridge Road, London SW1V 2SA

© 1998 by Sandra Glover

The right of Sandra Glover to be identified as the author of this
work has been asserted by her in accordance with the Copyright,
Designs and Patents Act, 1988

British Library Cataloguing in Publication Data available
ISBN 0 86264 854 8

Typeset by FSH, London WC1
Printed and bound in Great Britain by Mackays of Chatham PLC,
Chatham, Kent

Chapter 1

'Are you mad?' Elaine Dolby shouted.

She turned away from the staff room noticeboard and glared at Bryan Pugh.

'Er... no... I don't think so. Why?' said Mr Pugh. 'Is there a problem?'

'Suzie Lawrence,' said Mrs Dolby.

'Yes?' said Mr Pugh.

'You've got her on your work experience list.'

'Yes,' said Bryan Pugh, again. 'All the Year 10s are doing it. As they do every year. Two weeks to give them a taste of life in the big wide world. Barely adequate but an invaluable...'

'Don't lecture me, Bryan. I've worked in this school for thirty-one years and I'm well aware of what is done and why. It's not the idea of work experience I'm questioning. It's this particular placement. Suzie Lawrence, if my eyes don't deceive me, is down to work at the Manor.'

'Yes.'

'An old people's home.'

'Yes.'

'Mr Pugh,' she said, firmly. 'Do you teach Suzie Lawrence?'

'No.'

'Well, I do,' she announced triumphantly. 'Set 5 English. And I also have the dubious pleasure of entertaining Suzie in my tutor group, on her increasingly rare visits to school.'

'I know she's a poor attender,' said Mr Pugh. 'I had trouble tracking her down to arrange a placement at all...'

'You should have used a metal detector,' said Mrs Dolby, sweetly.

'Metal detector?'

'Mmmm. Stand on the corridor with one and tune in to Suzie's earrings and nose studs.'

'Okay, she wears jewellery,' said Mr Pugh, irritably. 'But I don't see...'

'Then let me spell it out for you. Suzie Lawrence is loud, foul-mouthed, aggressive, bone idle... and those are just her good points. She's the original pupil from hell and you're going to let her loose on a bunch of old dears with dodgy hearts.'

'Well it wasn't my first choice... or hers... In fact she didn't fancy anything but then she said she wouldn't mind trying hairdressing...'

'Hairdressing,' said Mrs Dolby. 'Well, yes, that sounds better... on the other hand... all those scissors...'

'But the head of science told me she had allergies to chemicals and stuff... brings her out all blotchy... I suggested office work but when I checked with some of her teachers they said her skills were too basic...'

'Nothing could be too basic for Suzie. My cat's got better communication skills.'

'So then Suzie said she fancied shop work... only

the secretary said she wasn't to be trusted round money...'

'How prejudiced of her,' said Elaine Dolby. 'Just because Suzie walked into the office and waltzed off with the dinner money last term... or perhaps she's still bleating about the time Suzie stole her handbag... but I suppose she could be right. Let's hope the old dears haven't got their life savings tucked under their mattresses.'

'Look,' said Mr Pugh. 'I'd be the first to admit it's difficult placing kids like Suzie. But we can't exclude them from the scheme just because they've got a few problems.'

'A few? Suzie brings a whole new definition to the word "problem". According to Suzie, rules are there to be broken. And if you'd bothered asking me, as you should have done, I could have told you.'

'It's poorly motivated children,' said Mr Pugh, ignoring the interruption, 'that the scheme is designed to help in the first place. Sometimes having a go at work makes them see the point of learning...'

'And sometimes pigs are seen flying over the playground.'

Bryan Pugh opened his mouth and closed it again. Maybe he'd be as bitter and cynical as Elaine Dolby after thirty-one years. As it was, he'd been teaching for barely three. And that was probably the root of the problem. Mrs Dolby was renowned for giving younger teachers a hard time. Especially ones who forgot to ask her opinion. Well, he was the careers teacher. It was his business.

3

'I'm sorry you don't approve,' he said at last.

'No, I don't,' said Mrs Dolby. 'Honestly you may as well send a shark to work in a swimming pool as send Suzie Lawrence to work in an old people's home. I only hope most of them are stone deaf or they'll be learning a whole new vocabulary.'

'I shouldn't think she'll have too much contact with the old people themselves,' said Mr Pugh, hopefully. 'It'll be mainly cleaning the floors and making the tea . . . '

'Yeees,' she drawled. 'I can just imagine them all frothing through their dentures.'

'What?'

'Oh, nothing. Just that three weeks ago Suzie was sent to the Head's office for some misdemeanour. Head was in a meeting with some governors so he asked Suzie to make the tea . . . save her sitting around doing nothing. Apparently she added a squirt of washing-up liquid . . . For someone who looks so . . . er . . . mature, she has a somewhat childish sense of humour does our Suzie. Still, I don't suppose she'll take her plastic spider with her . . . and Mrs Firth confiscated that dog pooh . . . Don't look so shocked. It wasn't real.'

'Are you making this up?' said Mr Pugh, catching a somewhat evil glint behind her spectacles.

'Bryan. With Suzie one doesn't need to make anything up. It's all there in her school records. We needed to upgrade the computer purely to accommodate them. But seriously, I do think you ought to change . . . '

'I can't,' said Mr Pugh. 'Even if I could think of anything more suitable. They start on Monday, and today, if you hadn't noticed, is Friday.'

'The thirteenth,' said Mrs Dolby.

'Anyway, you needn't worry. I'm going to supervise Suzie's placement myself.'

He tried to ignore the snort which burst forth from his colleague.

'Oh no you're not.'

'Pardon?'

'If,' said Elaine Dolby, glaring at him, 'you insist upon this madness, then I shall supervise Suzie's placement.'

To emphasise her point she picked up a pen, crossed his name off the list next to the Manor and replaced it with her own.

'And I warn you,' she added menacingly. 'If there is any problem... just one little death resulting from Suzie's actions, I shall recall her into school.'

Suzie Lawrence pulled the duvet cover up over her head, trying to ignore the Monday morning feeling which gnawed at her stomach.

'Go away,' she growled at the figure standing over her. 'I don't feel well. I aren't going to school today.'

Outside, on the landing, two small boys were fighting. Two girls burst into the bedroom.

'Mel,' one girl yelled. 'Jane's got my jumper on. I told her it's mine but she won't give it back.'

'This one's mine,' Jane screamed. 'Ellie's is in the dog's basket. Nick put it in last night 'cos he said the dog looked a bit cold.'

5

Melanie Johnson looked at the girls, at the boys rolling around on the carpet, at the heap under the duvet.

'Right,' she said. 'Nick. Pete. Go downstairs. Get your breakfast. NOW! Ellie, there's a spare jumper in the airing cupboard. Jane, go and rescue the other one from the dog...'

'Aw, but Mum, I didn't put it there...'

'No. But it would be a big help to me, if you got it out.'

'All right, Mum,' said Jane, revealing the huge gap where her two front teeth had recently been.

Melanie smiled. Some of these children she fostered called her Mum. Others didn't. Little Jane used the word almost obsessively. The heap under the duvet used it not at all.

'Come on, Suzie,' she said, pulling at the cover. 'It's not school today, anyway. You're doing work experience, remember?'

A head appeared. Brown, spiky, sleepy, like a hedgehog after a long hibernation.

'Nah. Don't fancy it,' said a voice as the head withdrew again.

'Suzie! You promised,' said Mel, appealing to the better nature she knew was buried under the cover along with the rest of Suzie Lawrence.

'Changed my mind.'

'Well, put it this way,' said Mel.

Reason and appeals were fine, when you had the time. Just at the moment, with the four younger ones squealing downstairs, Mel didn't. So she resorted to threats before leaving the room.

'No pocket money for a fortnight if you don't go.'

'Stupid cow,' said Suzie, throwing off the duvet and swinging her legs over the side of the bed. 'Who does she think she is?'

The question was not meant for anyone to answer. She knew exactly who Melanie Johnson was. Age 45. Mother of two grown-up children. Grandmother of twins. Experienced foster parent. Wife of Eric Johnson who worked for the electricity board and smiled a lot. They both smiled a lot. Him and Mel. Goodness knows what they had to smile about. House full of kids and animals. Five kids at the moment. Three cats. A dog. Tank of fish. Two rabbits. And the hamster Nick had brought with him from his last foster home.

Nick had come piled high with stuff. His last foster parents had been sorry to lose him but they had to move and Nick had to stay here. To be near his mum who came to see him sometimes.

None of these kids was actually an orphan. They all had at least one living parent. Parents who couldn't cope with them, for some reason or another. Nick was supposed to be going home soon. When his mum got a flat sorted out. And Pete was moving too. He was going to be adopted. That happened sometimes with the little ones.

Suzie pulled on her jeans and tee-shirt and headed for the bathroom. She splashed her face, staring at a spot on her forehead that had appeared from nowhere.

It was too late for her, of course. Nobody in their right mind wanted to adopt a spotty fourteen-year-old. Not that she was particularly spotty. Everyone said she was attractive. She supposed she must be. She was going out with Dave, wasn't she? And he only went for the good-looking girls. Anyway spots or no spots she was stuck with the Johnsons. Where she had been for the last three years. Or rather, they were stuck with her.

Yes, that was more like it, she thought, dabbing make-up onto the spot. At least they had stuck with her. Not like the others. She'd lost count of how many foster homes and children's homes she'd been in. Both before her mum died and after. Twenty? Thirty? More? Some had lasted barely a week before she'd been thrown out or run away.

'Suzie. Are you up yet?'

She didn't bother answering the call but stamped loudly back to the bedroom so Mel would get the message. She flopped on the bed. Ten more minutes before she had to go out. If she went.

She never bothered with breakfast so there was no hurry. Mel used to fuss about it. But that was in the days when Suzie barely ate at all and the doctor had muttered darkly about anorexia. Now she ate more than a swarm of locusts, Eric Johnson said. But never in the mornings. Mornings always made her feel sick.

It was bad this morning. Worse than when she was going to school. Or, more often, not going. If she couldn't pull a sicky, she'd go through the motions. Putting on a bit of uniform. Leaving the house. But, more often than not, she'd end up down town. Or at Dave's house. The school would phone Mel. There'd be bother when she got home. She'd promise to go the next day and the cycle would begin again.

And now, she had this new problem. She slipped on her boots and laced them up. May as well give it a try, this work experience lark. Couldn't be worse than school. On the other hand, her friend Gemma had told her it was a right con. She'd done it last year, in a florist's shop. Slave labour she called it. Sweeping leaves up off the floor and tidying shelves. She'd only stuck it two days. Said it was a waste of time and the people were foul.

Suzie wondered what the people at the Manor would be like. Old people could be right grumpy. She knew that because the woman next door, who was 68, was forever banging on the wall when Suzie played her CDs. And then there was the staff. If care workers were anything like social workers and teachers, they'd be dead bossy.

She groaned as she grabbed her jacket off the wardrobe door.

She didn't fancy it at all.

Chapter 2

The bus stopped right outside the Manor. Or rather outside the enormous stone wall which surrounded it. To get in you had to walk round the side, up a gravel slope and through the car park. Mr Pugh had told her that.

She kicked the gravel as she slouched along, wondering what she was doing here. It would be awful, she knew. Dave had fallen about laughing when she'd told him.

'You! Nursemaid to a load of barmy old wrinklies! You won't stick it five minutes.'

So why try at all? Why bother going in? Because she couldn't miss out on a fortnight's pocket money. That's why. Dave's birthday was coming up in three weeks. She wanted to get him something really nice and so far, she'd managed to save all of three pounds fifty! The Johnsons were pretty generous with money but it never seemed to stay in her purse for long. And then they had this stupid system of deductions if you mucked them around too much. And she'd been doing a lot of that, recently. Since she'd been seeing Dave.

'Blimey, looks worse than school this,' Suzie muttered, weaving her way through the cars.

She paused to look up at the grim Victorian building, then jumped as a car horn blasted in her ear. A bald man in a black saloon whizzed past her as she leapt out of the way.

She made a gesture at him, before moving on, towards the thick, double doors.

10

Inside, things immediately brightened. Suzie stepped into a corridor with yellow walls, a few pictures and a couple of low tables with magazines on. At the end of the corridor was a door labelled reception.

She didn't need to knock. The woman at the desk could see her through the glass panel and rose to meet her. She was shorter than Suzie. Quite plump. With an unruly mop of blonde curls which looked as though they should belong to a younger face. Not one like this with dry skin and middle-aged wrinkles, barely disguised beneath heavy make-up.

'You must be Suzie Lawrence,' she said letting her eyes explore from the top of Suzie's cropped hair to the tip of her thick, purple boots. 'I'm Jill Davis. Secretary. If you'd just like to have a seat and fill in a little form for me, I'll ring for Matron.'

Suzie sat down.

'Er... what do I write?'

'Well,' said Jill. 'You fill in your name where it says name. And your address where it says address... '

'Oh yeah. I get it.'

'Good,' said Jill picking up the phone.

Suzie tried to concentrate on her writing, as Jill spoke to Matron.

'Right. Matron will see you in her office. Bring the form.'

'But I haven't... '

Too late. Jill was already out of the door. Suzie grabbed the form, and followed. Jill gave a guided tour as they walked.

'Staff toilet. Kitchen where you can make lunch if you don't fancy the food here. And very few of us do. To be frank, I've seen better catering in a pigsty. Shouldn't say that really, should I? But it's all boiled rice and mashed vegetables. Yuk. Now that's the staff room... '

Suzie managed to glance in. It was bright and surprisingly modern. Maybe it wouldn't be too bad working in a place like this.

'You can spend your breaks in there, if you manage to get any. No smoking though... Here we are... '

She opened the door next to the staff room with the name Mrs Clarke, Matron, on it and abandoned Suzie to the grey-haired, unsmiling horror behind the desk.

'Sit down,' Matron said, without bothering with further pleasantries. 'Give me your form. Thank you. Muddlebunk... an unusual address, dear.'

'Middlebank,' said Suzie, leaning over the desk and pointing. 'That's an a and that's an i.'

'Ah, yes,' said Matron. 'If we put a dot over the top, it might help a bit. And join up the top of the a. Right. Now... date of birth.'

'You mean my birthday?'

'Yes, dear,' said Matron, rolling her bulbous eyes.

'August the ninth.'

'Ninth of the eighth,' Matron said as she wrote. 'Year?'

'Er... I'm fourteen... nearly fifteen.'

'Old enough to know your date of birth then,' Matron snapped, as she did a quick calculation and wrote down the year.

A knock on the door prevented Suzie from

responding. A dark-haired girl, in her early twenties, came in.

'Sorry to disturb you, Matron, but you said to call if there was any more trouble with Blind Bessie.'

As the girl spoke Suzie gazed round the enormous office, with its French windows leading out to a paved courtyard. Very nice this! They must be making a packet.

'Yes. Yes. I'll deal with her. Honestly, as if I didn't have enough to do without Blind Bessie kicking up a fuss again. Take Suzie with you. We'll fill the form in later.'

Matron hurried from the room leaving Suzie with the young woman.

'Hi. I'm Trish. Come on then. You can help me do the beds.'

They headed through a maze of corridors until they came to a lift.

'We start on the top floor. Men's rooms. And work down,' Trish explained.

She pushed open the door of the first room and flicked on the light. Suzie was surprised at how small it was. And dark. Even with the light on.

'Not very nice,' Suzie muttered, tugging at a piece of loose wallpaper.

'Leave it alone,' Trish snapped.

'Are all the rooms like this?' she asked, looking at the cracked sink in the corner.

'You'll see,' said Trish, as she got to work.

They were. In fact, some were much worse. Flimsy,

torn curtains. Stains on the walls. Scratches on the furniture.

'Er...' said Suzie, as they moved out of the fourth room. 'Where are the...er...old people? I haven't seen...'

'Oh, you will in a minute,' said Trish. 'Most of them are down in the lounge by now. But we have a few who are bedridden. Mr Pole's in number 36, here.'

Suzie looked at the name on the door plate.

'It says Mr Kona... Konask...'

'Exactly,' said Trish. 'Polish and unpronounceable. So we settle for Mr Pole. Doesn't make any difference to him. Deaf as a post.'

In the event, Suzie didn't meet Mr Pole.

'Dr Grenville's with him,' Trish said, having poked her head round the door. 'Had another of his turns, I expect. Mr Pole, not Dr Grenville.'

By the time they had finished both floors, Suzie had seen three old people, all fast asleep, and was trying not to envy them as she yawned and stretched to ease her aching back.

'Right,' said Trish. 'Time to do the elevenses. We'll grab a coffee while we're doing it. There's no chance of a proper break.'

'No break!' said Suzie, horrified.

'Can't when we're short staffed,' said Trish. 'Which is more or less all the time. There's always people leaving. Then it takes a couple of weeks to replace them. So if anyone's on a sicky, you're stuck. Lucky we've got you this week, really. You'll be a big help.'

14

'That's what she thinks,' Suzie muttered.

'Where are you going? Not that way.'

They were back on the ground floor and Suzie had headed towards the kitchen she had seen earlier.

'That's the staff kitchen. Big kitchen's downstairs.'

'Downstairs?'

'In the basement. Next to the residents' lounge.'

'Residents' lounge?' Suzie repeated. 'You keep the old people in the basement!'

The basement was darker and dingier than the bedrooms with corridors painted putrid green. The kitchen was made bright by fluorescent strips which cast garish light onto the pale tiles.

Two middle-aged ladies in white overalls and caps were busy chopping vegetables.

'Annie and Pat,' said Trish. 'This is Suzie. Work experience.'

'Yes, well, it's definitely an experience working here, luv,' said Annie.

'Grab some cups from over there, while I put the kettle on, will you, Suzie,' said Trish.

Suzie picked up a cup. Replaced it. Got another one. Put it back.

'Come on, luv,' said Annie. 'We want them for morning break, not supper.'

'I'm tryin' to find some without cracks in,' said Suzie.

'You'll be lucky,' said Pat. 'This is the Manor not the bloody Ritz.'

'But ... they might cut themselves or ... Mel always says cracks harbour germs.'

'Hark at her!' said Pat. 'I don't know who this Mel is, luv, but her rules don't apply here. Now be a good girl and get the cups on that tray, will yer. I need the work surface.'

'Can I use these?' said Suzie, spotting some healthier looking specimens on a high shelf.

'No you can't,' said Annie. 'Those are for visitors. If you give them out they'll get dropped and broken like the rest.'

'But...'

'This is your first day, right?' said Annie.

Suzie nodded, sullenly.

'Well try not to make it your last, eh? Just do what you're told and stop causing bother.'

'Bother?' Suzie muttered, slamming some cups onto the tray. 'You 'aven't seen nothin', if you think this is bother.'

But she said it to herself. Not loudly as she would have done at school. She didn't intend to waste much more time here, breaking her back and being ordered around. Pocket money or no pocket money. But she wasn't going yet. Not until she'd met the old people. She just had to see the poor inmates of this depressing hole before she left.

16

Chapter 3

'You wouldn't believe it,' said Suzie, in answer to Mel's question later that evening.

'Not too good, eh?'

'Good it's f...'

'Suzie!'

'Flamin' awful. Gemma was right. This work experience is a right con. I never stopped all day. Cleaning bedrooms, mopping floors, loading the dish washer. And did I get any thanks? Oh no! It's all hurry up, Suzie. That's not very clean, Suzie. Do it again, Suzie.'

'Oh dear,' said Mel. 'You didn't...'

'Nah, I was dead good,' said Suzie. 'I didn't even swear when that stupid cow of a Matron told me to stop chatting an' get on with clearing up the lunch plates. You're not allowed to talk to 'em, you know? The old folk. There's no bloody time. Shovel the food in. Whip the plates away. Turn the telly on. Hope the poor old dears doze off.'

'Well elderly people do need a lot of sleep.'

'They get it whether they need it or not. There's nowt else to do. I tell you, I don't ever want to get old, like that. It's a great advert for booze, drugs and cigarettes, is that place. May as well live a bit, while you've got the chance. What's the point of doin' all that clean livin' stuff, if you're gonna end up a wreck, anyhow? I reckon my mum had it right.'

'Suzie. How can you say that?'

'I just have.'

'Your mum was only twenty-six when she...'

'I know that.'

'Maybe you don't remember...'

'I remember it! All of it,' Suzie snapped. 'I weren't a kid! I were eight. It were me that phoned for the ambulance. I were with her...'

'I'm sorry,' said Mel as Suzie brushed her sleeve across her eyes. 'I shouldn't have...'

'It don't matter,' said Suzie. 'But I tell you. I'd throw myself under a bus rather than end up in a hole like that.'

'Mel,' yelled Nick bursting into the room. 'Are you takin' me to Cubs or what?'

'I thought you weren't going any more. I thought you said it was naff.'

'Yeah... well... they're doin' sausages tonight. On a camp fire.'

'I see,' said Mel. 'I'll take the others with me, Suzie. They've had tea. You can have some chicken tikka with me and Eric later. Give it a stir, will you? I won't be long.'

Suzie did as instructed and headed upstairs to have a bath, pouring in half a bottle of bath foam in an attempt to ease her aches and pains.

She lay back in the water. Feet up. Toes curled round the taps. What a day! She was surprised to find herself thinking about it. Usually, when she got home from school, that was it. She never gave it a second thought, unless Mel was on one of her campaigns to get her to do

18

homework. But this was different. She couldn't get the Manor out of her head.

It had been a real shock walking into that basement lounge. In fact, she'd crashed the drinks trolley into a table and Trish had yelled at her. But you could hardly help banging the trolley against something or other. The lounge was quite big, but dark and full of obstacles. Armchairs, wheelchairs, tables, television, foot-stools and various bits and pieces that had been dropped on the floor. And the feet, of course. Dozens of pairs of feet stretched out. Some wrapped in rugs. Others in faded slippers or flat shoes.

Wrinkled, twisted, deformed feet belonging to wrinkled, twisted, deformed people with grey faces and eyes that stared blankly into time and space.

Suzie shivered. It had been like walking onto the set of some old horror film. *Return of the Zombies. Night of the Living Dead.* No, worse than that. Old movies didn't have smells. The lounge did. Stale sweat, urine and the hint of food that might be quietly rotting along with the people.

She'd wanted to turn and run. But she couldn't. Partly because Trish had already stuck a teapot in her hand and partly because she'd been drawn to the old people by a sort of morbid curiosity.

The first guy she'd tried to serve had nodded continually.

'Don't give him sugar,' Trish had said.

'But I asked him and he nodded . . .'

'Yes he would,' said Trish. 'Nodding Ned, we call

19

him. Always nodding, aren't you, love?' she asked, loudly.

Ned had nodded aqain.

'Never speaks,' said Trish. 'No reason why he can't. He just doesn't. Never speak, do you, Ned?'

Suzie cringed. All the staff were like that. They all adopted sickly, sugary voices which masked a hint of menace when they spoke to the old people. Worse than the teachers at school.

'Now we don't do that, do we, Suzie?'

Fancy putting up with all that rot when you're a kid, only to face it all again before you were allowed to die, Suzie thought, slamming her feet into the water, watching it cascade over the side of the bath.

At least you didn't have to take it at school. She didn't anyway. But the old folks – what could they do about it? Couldn't walk out, could they? No wonder Ned had stopped speaking. What was the point? Nobody listened. They didn't have time.

There was one old lady who had really wanted to chat. That's when Matron had walked in.

'Suzie! It's half past one. Didn't Trish tell you we have lunch cleared away by one fifteen?'

'Yes but I was just talking to . . . '

'Blind Bessie. I know. But if you let her start, she'll keep you there all day. Suzie has to get on, Bessie,' Matron had said, as if addressing a total imbecile. 'You have a nice chat to Elsie instead.'

'Elsie's senile,' Bessie had whispered to Suzie. 'You can't have a proper conversation with her. She doesn't know what you're saying. Most of 'em don't. That's why they're in here. Because they're barmy.'

Suzie had looked at one old lady, who was humming a Christmas carol whilst happily crumbling a biscuit onto the carpet, and acknowledged that Bessie was probably right.

'I'm not though,' Bessie insisted. 'I've still got all my marbles. Couldn't cope when I lost my eyesight, though. Not like when you're blind from birth. When it happens suddenly, like it did with me, you're a bit lost. Went two years ago, my eyes did. I was 73. I didn't look it in those days. My neighbour used to say I didn't look a day over sixty. Bet I do now,' she added, wrinkling her nose. 'This place is enough to put years on anyone. Good job I can't see myself.'

Suzie hadn't known what to say. Bessie looked old to her. White, lank hair dangling round her ears. The yellowish pallor which might have been a result of the poor lighting.

'Look at this thing they keep giving me to wear,' said Bessie, fingering a green cardigan with holes in the sleeves. 'I've got nice clothes but they say I'll get them dirty. Spill my food. But I wouldn't. Wouldn't do anything else either. Not like some ... Elsie's got no bowel control ...'

'Suzie!' Matron had yelled. 'How many times do I have to tell you? Clear those plates away.'

So Suzie had never got to hear the details of Elsie's bowels. Bessie had whispered one more thing to her before she had to go but it wasn't about Elsie's bowels.

Still, thought Suzie, as she climbed out of the bath and started to get dressed, it must be rotten for them. The ones who couldn't control their bowels and bladders. Peeing all over the place would be bad enough. But to have everyone knowing about it! Talking about it!

Suzie shuddered and tried to forget. Easy for the next hour with Mel and the kids back. Suzie even helped get the little ones ready for bed. Suddenly their runny noses and smelly feet didn't seem so bad any more.

When Eric got home, it started all over again. Not exactly the sort of thing you wanted to discuss over the chicken tikka, so Suzie tried to concentrate on the less gory bits.

'It's a right funny place,' she said in answer to his opening question. 'It looks dead good when you walk in. Flowers and pictures all over the place. But they keep the old folks in the bloody basement . . .'

'Suzie!' warned Mel.

'I only said bloody. I mean, the whole place makes you want to swear. It's a right pigsty, that basement. And when I asked, Trish said it weren't worth decorating or owt 'cos they'd only muck it up. Then I said, they could at least 'ave a few flowers to brighten the place up. And then Annie stuck her fat nose in an' told me it were none of my business . . .'

'Is she still alive?' said Eric.

'I just ignored her.'

'Things are improving,' said Eric.

Suzie laughed. She didn't mind when Eric said things like that. He was the sort of person it was hard to get mad with. He had a chubby face, with a stupid grin which made him look more like a kid than a proper adult.

'Yeah, well,' she said, as though she felt she had to apologise for avoiding a confrontation. 'I couldn't be bothered arguing. I was too knackered by that time. You know they're supposed to have twelve day staff and I only saw five today... and me. And Matron does nowt apart from come round moaning every five minutes.'

'Welcome to the world of work,' said Eric and proceeded to complain about his boss for the next half hour.

'Yeah, I get the message,' said Suzie. 'But at least you get paid for what you do. I mean, Trish told me what she gets an' it's pathetic. And I don't get nowt at all.'

'I'll double your pocket money,' Eric announced, 'if you stick at it for the whole fortnight.'

Suzie did some rather slow, painful, mental arithmetic.

'Thirty quid?'

'If you like,' said Eric.

'Why?' said Suzie, knowing from Eric's eyes she was being conned. 'Is it more than that?'

'Maths can come in handy sometimes.'

'So. Okay. I'm thick...'

'You're not thick, Suzie.'

'Is it forty?'

Eric nodded.

Suzie considered the possibilities of having forty pounds in her pocket in two weeks' time. She could buy

Dave a really decent present with that.

'Trouble is,' she said, almost to herself. 'I don't think I can. I mean, honest, Eric. You wouldn't neither, if you'd seen the place. I reckon it's gonna give me nightmares. I nearly bunked off this afternoon only Harry started cryin' after Pat yelled at him for spillin' his drink. An' after I'd cleaned 'im up, I didn't like to just leave 'im...'

'It can't be that bad,' said Mel. 'If it's constantly under-staffed and the old people aren't being looked after properly, somebody would be onto them. These private nursing homes have to meet certain standards, you know.'

'So do prisons,' said Suzie. 'But that don't mean I'd like to live or work in one. I mean I reckon I've already done it anyway.'

'Done what?' said Mel.

'What Mr Pugh said. He said, we were meant to try a kind of work to see if it's what you'd like to do when you leave school. Well, I 'ave and it isn't.'

Melanie and Eric looked at each other across the table. This sounded like one of Suzie's many arguments about why she needn't bother going to school. They both felt a sense of defeat that no amount of extra pocket money was going to change. Either they could dig in for a long daily battle or give up gracefully now.

Suzie yawned.

'I think I'll have an early night.'

'You're not going out?' asked Mel, amazed.

'Nah, I'm knackered. And besides, Dave phoned and

said he was off to his dad's for a couple of days.'

She saw Mel and Eric frown at the mention of Dave's name. They didn't like Dave. They said it was because he was nineteen and too old for her. But it wasn't just that. They could be right snobbish, Mel and Eric. Fussing because Dave had a few tattoos and had been in a bit of bother with the cops.

Suzie shrugged. It didn't matter what they thought. They couldn't stop her seeing him.

'Night, then,' she said. 'Oh, an' give us a shout early tomorrow, will you, Mel?'

'Er yes ... but ... I mean ... I thought you weren't ...'

'Well I don't know whether I'll stick two weeks of it,' said Suzie. 'But I've got to go tomorrow. I promised Bessie I'd do somethin' for her, see?'

Chapter 4

Melanie hadn't invested too much hope in Suzie's statement of the previous night. There was a saying, 'The road to hell is paved with good intentions', which could have been invented especially for Suzie. Not that she was a bad kid. Considering.

According to her records, Suzie had spent the first eight years of her life with a mother who doted on her but who could barely look after herself, let alone a child. Suzie's father had disappeared long before the birth. Her mother drifted in and out of relationships, sometimes ending up in a refuge for battered women. Often in hospital after injuries, drug overdoses and two miscarriages. Sometimes Suzie went with her. At other times she was taken into care. Only then did she mix with other children or go to school on a regular basis.

Angry and confused when her mother died, Suzie had failed to settle anywhere. In the first three months she was with them, Melanie had seen why. Suzie had broken up furniture, run away at least twice a week, kicked Eric and tried to strangle the cat. She'd also cried a lot, said she was sorry and clung to Mel like her life depended on it. Which, in a way, it did.

Suzie was still difficult. Perhaps the most difficult child Mel had ever had to deal with. But her intentions were always good. True, there was a gap the size of the Grand Canyon between what she intended and what she actually did. Making promises to little old ladies wouldn't exactly count for much with Suzie.

'I'm off now!'

Mel froze, the box of cereal in her hand, poised above Nick's bowl.

'I said I'm goin',' Suzie repeated.

Melanie glanced at the clock. It wasn't even eight o'clock, the time she would normally start to rouse Suzie.

'Oh... right... do you need anything...?'

But Mel was talking to herself. Suzie had gone.

Luckily all the bedrooms had nameplates outside. Suzie had crept into the Manor. Not many people to avoid at that time of day. There had only been three cars in the car park. One was the black saloon that had almost knocked her over the previous day. She had seen the top of a bald head hidden behind a newspaper and vaguely wondered who the man was, before slipping in at a side door to avoid passing reception.

She didn't bother knocking. No point attracting attention.

'Bessie?' she said, switching on the light and drawing back the curtains from the tiny window.

The light wouldn't make any difference to Bessie. Good job, really. You'd get more out of a glowworm than you would out of that feeble bulb.

'Suzie? Is that you?'

'Yeah. Said I'd come, didn't I?'

Bessie sat up and swung her feet over the side of the bed with more life and energy than Suzie usually managed.

Some clothes, including the cardigan from the previous day, had been thrown over the arm of a chair.

'Right,' said Suzie, ignoring them. 'Let's have a look in the wardrobe.'

'Is my green dress still there?' said Bessie. 'I remember I had a lovely green dress with a sort of stripe in it.'

'Er...can't see anything green...'

'I knew some of it was missing,' said Bessie. 'I told them. I used to have dozens of dresses and skirts and jumpers.'

'There's a sort of tweedy skirt,' said Suzie. 'That's nice.'

Not that it was the sort of thing she'd wear or even Mel but she guessed it was nice, in its own way.

'Now let's see what we've got in the drawers. Hey, this is okay,' she said picking up a white jumper and describing it to Bessie. 'It's dead soft. Here. Have a feel.'

'I don't know,' said Bessie, nervously. 'It's white, you say? They don't like us to wear white. They say it stains and is a devil to wash. But I remember the one... It's lovely on.'

'Well wear it then,' said Suzie, recalling her own battles about nose studs at school. 'They can't stop you. It's yours, in't it? An' if it gets a bit grubby I'll take it home. Mel'll wash it. You should see the stains she gets out of Pete's school shirts. Blimey! I sound like an advert for Persil or somatt, don't I?'

'Who's Mel, dear?'

'My mum.'

'And you call her Mel,' said Bessie. 'Things have changed since my day.'

'Yeah, well,' said Suzie, reluctant to go into details. 'The younger generation, eh?'

'They can't be too bad, if they're all like you.'

Suzie laughed. If only Bessie knew!

She handed over the clothes.

'I'll pop along to the bathroom first. Don't worry. I can manage. Just put the clothes under my arm and pass me my stick.'

'Nasty bruise that,' said Suzie, pointing to Bessie's wrist as she put the stick in her hand.

'Is it?' said Bessie. 'I thought it might have come up a bit. It's very sore. They shouldn't grab you like that, you know.'

'What d'you mean?'

'It was one of the night staff, saying I was being awkward. Trying to hurry me up. She squeezed my wrist when she grabbed me ... I told her ... '

'You ought to complain!' said Suzie. 'Have you told Matron?'

'No point. Half the time they don't believe you. And even if they do it's hard to prove,' said Bessie, opening the door.

Suzie sat on the end of the bed, kicking her legs. Didn't old people have any rights or what? Teachers weren't allowed to do that to kids. So why should Bessie have to put up with it?

She idly picked up a purse which was lying on the

bedside cabinet and opened it. Not much there. A few coins and a five-pound note. She closed it and pulled down the wallet section. A dry cleaning ticket. A library ticket. From ages back, both of them, she reckoned. She flicked through other bits of paper. It never occurred to her that there was anything wrong. That this was private property.

A photograph. She took it out. A baby. Grandchild? Son? Daughter? No. Couldn't be. Bessie was a Miss. Miss Elizabeth Bradshaw it said on the door. Bessie herself? Could be. The photograph looked as old as everything else tucked away there.

She put it back. Prowled round the room. Opened a few drawers. Not a lot to show for seventy... what was it Bessie had said... seventy-five years.

Bessie was taking a long time. Suzie opened the bedroom door and picked up a newspaper that was lying outside, just as Bessie came back.

'There's a newspaper here. *The Times*.'

'Yes, dear. Bring it in.'

'But...'

'I order one every day... sometimes somebody reads me a bit...but mostly they don't. I've got a few talking books to keep me going and I get a weekly newspaper on tape...but I don't know. I guess it's a habit...'

'You look nice,' said Suzie.

'I feel nice,' said Bessie. 'Are you any good at crosswords?'

'Never done one.'

'I miss the crosswords. Read me some clues.'

30

'Er... I don't read too good,' said Suzie, trying to unravel the paper, to find the right page.

'We'll manage,' said Bessie. 'You can spell words out if you get stuck. What's one across?'

They did quite well, or rather Bessie did, despite the handicap of Suzie's reading.

'You've got some lipstick, in the drawer, you know,' said Suzie as her concentration started to wander. 'Shall I put you some on?'

'Why not?' said Bessie, not even questioning how Suzie knew the contents of the drawer.

'Suzie!'

Suzie's hand never wavered as the door burst open and Trish came in.

'I've come to take Bessie down... what on earth...'

'She wanted me to come early and help her find some decent clothes,' said Suzie, defiantly.

'Matron'll do her nut,' said Trish. 'They're supposed to keep their best stuff for when they've got visitors coming.'

'I bet they are!'

'It makes sense,' Trish said, dropping her voice. 'I mean she can't even see...'

'But I can hear...'

'Sorry,' said Trish. 'But you know what Matron...'

'Oh, dear,' said Bessie. 'Suzie isn't going to get into trouble, is she? It was my fau...'

'No it wasn't and I'm not,' said Suzie. 'If anybody says owt, I'll tell 'em. An you tell 'em too. They're your clothes. You can wear what you like. You've a right to

31

look decent. In fact, I'm gonna do your hair later, Bessie. Where can I find some rollers?'

'Rollers?' said Trish. 'When do you think you're going to have time...'

'I'll make time,' Suzie snarled. 'You get me the rollers and I'll find the time.'

'Matron...'

'Yeah, yeah. I know. Matron'll throw a wobbler. Well, I'm used to people throwin' wobblers so it won't make no odds to me. And Bessie aren't scared of no Matron, are you, Bess? How much d'you pay for this place then?'

'Oh boy,' said Trish, rolling her eyes. 'Where did they find you from?'

Suzie barely saw Trish for the rest of the day. Trish was assigned to rooms and Suzie to help Annie in the kitchen. Pat was off sick. At half past four when Suzie was putting some rather unappetising cheese spread sandwiches on a plate for tea, Trish popped her head round the door.

'Someone to see you in Matron's office, Suzie.'

'To see me? Who?'

'A Mrs Dolby from school.'

Suzie wiped her hands on the white overall she'd been given and left Trish and Annie to the sandwiches. What on earth was Mrs Dolby doing here? It was only Tuesday. Teachers weren't supposed to come till the end of the week. Then it was supposed to be Mr Pugh. Typical of Mrs Dolby though to come snooping. Well, she was going to be disappointed. She'd been dead good

32

these past two days, Suzie thought, confidently knocking on Matron's door.

They looked an odd pair, Matron and Mrs Dolby, sitting on opposite sides of the desk, like distorted mirror images. Both grey-haired and in their fifties. Matron, large, thick-set with eyes that stuck out, like a frog's. Mrs Dolby, tall, eyes sunk into a thin, sharp face.

Matron pointed to a vacant seat next to Mrs Dolby.

'I thought I'd pop in and see how you were doing, Suzie.'

'I'm doin' great.'

The two women looked at each other.

'Er... Matron tells me there have been one or two problems.'

'Like what?'

'Like,' said Matron, 'disappearing for an hour after lunch when you were supposed to be washing up.'

'I didn't disappear. I went to do Bessie's hair.'

'Blind Bessie,' said Matron to Mrs Dolby, 'is a rather manipulative woman. Always complaining about...'

'Do you have to?' said Suzie.

'Pardon?' said Matron.

'Do you have to talk about 'em like that? Blind Bessie. Nodding Ned. Mr Pole! Labels. It's worse than bloody school. Suzie, Set 5. Kate, Set 1. Labels, not people. See?'

Mrs Dolby saw. She would have cheered aloud if Suzie had managed to say anything so articulate or analytical in an English lesson. As it was, with Matron scowling, she didn't know quite what to say.

33

'You see what I mean?' said Matron, ignoring Suzie completely. 'It's an attitude problem. Suzie doesn't like being told what to do. She likes to go her own way. It might work at school but it won't work at the Manor. We're a team here.'

'Crap,' said Suzie. 'You can't keep your staff for five minutes. They're overworked, knackered, bad-tempered and too scared to say or do owt about it . . . '

'Well, if that's how you feel,' said Matron, 'I can see there is no point you staying on.'

Chapter 5

'It's not fair,' said Suzie, taking off one of her boots and throwing it across the lounge.

'Suzie,' said Mel. 'You nearly hit Nick's head then. Now calm down.'

'Well, it's not. If Mrs Dolby hadn't come snooping around, Matron wouldn't have started on me. I were doin' all right.'

'But...'

'The old folks like me,' said Suzie, defiantly. 'Even Elsie, who doesn't know what bloody planet she's on, smiles when I talk to her. And I got her to answer me properly today. Stick to the conversation. We managed half a dozen sentences before she started ramblin'.'

'So...'

'It's her. Matron. She's got it in for me. Told Mrs Dolby I talk too much. I can't follow instructions. I break all the rules. I'm stroppy...'

'Well...'

'But I 'aven't bin. That's the point. I got all the work done and found time to...'

'Now wait a minute,' said Mel, determined to get in more than single words. 'What happened after Matron told you it wasn't worth you staying on?'

'I give 'er a piece of my mind, didn't I? Had to, didn't I?'

'Not necessarily... there are ways of handling situations.'

'That's what Mrs Dolby said. You're all alike you are. Put up with anythin'. But I won't. And Dave agrees. He says...'

'But from what you told me when you came in, Mrs Dolby was on your side,' said Mel hastily, before Suzie could repeat any little gems that had come from Dave's mouth.

'You don't listen, do you?' Suzie snapped. 'She weren't on my side at all. Sure she persuaded Matron to let me stay on. Givin' me another chance, she called it. But Matron wouldn't 'ave agreed if they weren't so short staffed. And Mrs Dolby! She were only doin' it 'cos of her precious school. Don't look too good when kids are thrown out of work experience. There were hell on last year when only half made it to the end.'

'All right,' said Mel. 'For whatever reasons, they're letting you stay on. And you want to, yes?'

'Yeah. It's okay, really. Better than school. And I 'ad fun today. Me 'an Bessie 'ad a right laugh when I took lunch round. It were Spotted Dick for puddin'. It'd gone cold and the custard was all lumpy and Bessie said...'

Mel smiled. She had never seen Suzie as animated about anything as she was about these old people. Maybe she identified with them in their helplessness. Being pushed around, as Suzie put it. Whatever the reason, this could be good for Suzie. If only she could keep her mouth in check.

Mel's words came back into Suzie's head, on Wednesday morning, as she walked through the car park.

'Remember, now, Suzie. Engage brain before opening mouth.'

There was no black saloon today with its bald-headed occupant. But it had been there last night when Suzie had stormed out. Who was he? With any luck he'd be some official checking up on the place. But what good could you do lurking outside? You'd have to work in the place to see the muck they were given to eat, and hear how some of the staff spoke to the old folks!

As she passed Matron's office she saw a couple of blokes in smart suits. Maybe they were officials. Somebody ought to check on this place, that was for sure.

She was still thinking about it while she was serving breakfast with Pat, who had rapidly recovered from whatever had kept her off the previous day.

'Not toast!' Pat snapped, snatching a plate from under a man's nose. 'I told you, Noddy has cereal!'

'What's his name?' said Suzie. 'His proper name.'

'Ned.'

'His proper name,' Suzie insisted.

'Edward Tyler,' said Pat. 'Why?'

Tyler. Edward Tyler. The name rang a bell but Suzie couldn't think where she'd heard it before. No, not heard it. She'd seen it. Written down. Probably on his bedroom door.

'Here you are, then, Mr Tyler,' said Suzie. 'Rice Krispies. D'you like Krispies?'

He nodded.

'Good job, really, aren't it?' said Suzie smiling. 'You don't exactly get a choice, do you?'

He nodded again.

'If you'd like something else, you just say, now. And I'll see what I can do.'

'You'll be lucky,' said Pat. 'He hasn't spoken these last five years and at ninety he's hardly likely to start now, is he? Mrs S will have toast, won't you, Mrs S?'

'Doesn't anyone 'ave a proper name around here?' said Suzie, passing the toast to a lady in a faded print dress.

'Smith's a common name,' said Pat. 'We had three Mrs Smiths when she first came. So we called her Mrs S. Other two have died now so it doesn't much matter.'

The casual mention of death made Suzie shudder.

'What do you liked to be called?' she asked.

'Lily... that's what my husband used to call me. I like Lily.'

'Right, Lily. Cup of tea?'

'I'll have to go and start lunch now,' said Pat when all the breakfasts had been served. 'Shouldn't really leave you without a qualified member of staff but needs must. Put the pots on the tray and give me a shout when it's all done.'

Suzie wandered round, straightening up cushions, rearranging blankets, chatting as she went.

'You look nice, Bessie. Did you do what I said? Did you tell 'em?'

'Yes, dear, I did. And I got Barbara to do the same,' she said pointing to a lady who was rather more smartly dressed than she had been on previous days. 'I'm working on Lily Smith next. But the trouble is she

38

doesn't remember. Tell her now and it's gone two minutes later.'

'We'll make a rebel of you yet, Bessie,' said Suzie.

'Oh, I always was a bit of a rebel, dear,' said Bessie. 'But it doesn't always do, you know. Gets you into trouble. Trouble you regret for the rest of your life...'

The crash interrupted them and Suzie had to scurry over to pick up Mr Vincent's cup.

'Sorry,' he said.

'You don't 'ave to say that. It were an accident.'

Suzie smiled at him. Smiled at herself. It was weird the effect these old people had on her. She didn't seem to get mad with them no matter what they did or said. Some of them were right moaners but she didn't yell at them like she did at her teachers. How could you? They were so helpless. So sad. Trapped in bodies which barely worked any more.

'My hands shake so much, you see,' Mr Vincent said, holding one out for inspection.

'Never mind. It don't matter.'

'I can't draw any more,' he said, wistfully.

'You like drawin', do you?'

'I was good. Drew cartoons for the newspapers. Not now though. Takes me all my time to draw breath.'

This was accompanied by a throaty laugh, followed by a cough. Suzie patted his back, as she had seen Mel do with the little ones.

'Bessie likes her newspapers,' she said, an idea coming into her head. 'You ought to sit next to Bessie. Have a chat.'

39

'Bessie sits in the corner,' he said, as though it were a fixture for life.

'Well, let's see if we can wheel you across, shall we?'

It was hard work, steering his wheelchair across the lumpy carpet. Moving Elsie back a bit. Creating a bit of space for Lily to squeeze in but it was worth it. Suzie stood back and admired her efforts. That was much better. If she could just move Edward Tyler into the circle...

'What on earth is going on?'

Suzie swung round at the sound of Matron's voice.

She stood in the doorway, hands on fat hips. The two men in suits standing behind her.

'I'm sorry,' she said to them. 'The work experience girl I told you about. Why have you been left in here on your own? It's almost eleven. Why haven't the breakfast pots been cleared? And what's that on the floor? Tea. Get a cloth and clear it up!'

'I were going to,' said Suzie, grabbing a cloth off the trolley. 'I've just bin moving people round a bit.'

'So I see! Well you can just move them back again.'

'Why?'

'Because they all have their places, that's why. It confuses them to be moved around.'

'How do you know?' said Suzie, wiping up the tea and standing up to face Matron. 'Have you asked them?'

'No but I happen to have been working in residential homes for thirty years. And in this particular one for five. Unlike you, my dear, who have been here barely three days.'

'I know but...'

Engage brain before opening mouth.

Mel's advice stopped Suzie in her tracks.

'Perhaps,' said Matron, 'I could introduce you to Dr Grenville and Mr Forest. They own the Manor. I'm sure they'd be interested in some of your revolutionary opinions.'

The two men stepped forward. The younger one with the blue suit and even bluer eyes extended his hand.

'Dr Grenville and this is my business partner, Mr Forest.'

Having been taught by Mrs Dolby, Suzie should have grasped the concept of sarcasm but Matron's had escaped her. This was better than people checking up. These were the owners. Surely they'd want to know what was going on?

'Hi,' she said. 'Well, I suppose it's okay here, but I reckon half of the people are bored to death, see? That's why I moved 'em round. So they could talk to each other. And to be honest, it's a bit of a mess down here, aren't it?'

'Excuse me?' said Mr Forest, waddling towards her.

His tone should have warned Suzie that he was not entirely open minded on the subject.

'It could do with decoratin', couldn't it? An' a new carpet. I mean it's barely worth moppin' up tea stains. Talk about threadbare... there's even a hole under t' table there.'

'And have you any idea how much your little scheme might cost?' Mr Forest asked. 'I'm not made of money, you know.'

41

He looked as though he might be with his red face, fat stomach, immaculate clothes and expensive leather shoes.

'No. But I reckon you can afford it. Bessie says she pays...'

'Does she now,' said Dr Grenville, glaring at her.

A pointless gesture, as Bessie couldn't see, of course.

'I don't suppose she tells you what she gets for her money, does she?' said Mr Forest. 'Food, board, qualified care day and night... It doesn't come cheap, you know.'

'Yeah,' said Suzie. 'But times that by... how many people have you got here?'

'Forty-four.'

Suzie knew she hadn't a hope of timesing anything by forty-four, so she changed tactics.

'And you found the money for upstairs, didn't you? Matron's office an' reception. No mouldy old carpets up there.'

'First impressions are important,' said Mr Forest.

'Who to?' said Suzie. 'Visitors? The relatives who are shelling out the money? I don't suppose the residents get to see much of it, do they? Goin' up and down in them lifts.'

'No, we don't,' someone muttered.

'An' it's us that has to live here...'

'I had to sell my house, in the end,' said Harry, starting to cry. 'Only way I could afford to...'

'See what you've done?' Matron snapped. 'You've got them all worked up. It'll play havoc with their blood

42

pressure. These old people are my responsibilty, Suzie. They'll be my responsibility long after you've gone back to school. I won't have them upset.'

She stopped suddenly as Elsie started to cough.

'See what you've done,' said Matron, hurrying over to Elsie with Dr Grenville.

'Don't look so worried,' said Mr Forest. 'That wasn't your fault. Elsie suffers with her chest. These coughing fits happen all the time. But Matron's right. She does a brilliant job keeping our residents calm and settled. It doesn't do to get them all worked up. And as for your other points, my dear, we provide an excellent service here, for what we charge. We're much cheaper than some of the other homes and we look into the few complaints we get very carefully.'

'Yeah, but ...'

'And, as it happens, redecoration of the residents' lounge is on our list for improvement after re-surfacing the car park. When we've got the money, of course. Which we haven't at the moment, as I keep pointing out to Matron, when she asks for extra staff and new curtains for the bedrooms. But you see, it's all under control.'

'Keep my mouth shut, in other words,' said Suzie. 'Where have I heard that before?'

Then, a little quieter.

'Gemma and Dave were right. I'm out of here.'

She tried to phone Dave that night but he was still down south with his dad who wasn't on the phone. Gemma was out too. Her mum said she hadn't seen her

43

for a couple of days. So Suzie stamped around the house, told Mel she'd quit the Manor, had a massive row, went to bed and by the time she got up, had changed her mind.

Okay, so she didn't like Matron or the idea of the owners getting rich at the residents' expense but going to the Manor would at least get her out of the house. And the longer she stuck it the more money she'd get. No small matter with Dave's birthday coming up. Besides, she'd had an idea for livening things up a bit.

Chapter 6

Suzie plonked some carnations in a vase and pulled back the basement curtains as far as they would go.

So the owners hadn't exactly been keen on her ideas. What did she expect when they were clearly only in it for the money? But they couldn't stop her talking to the old folk and bringing in some flowers.

Whether the neighbours would be pleased when they noticed their carnations were missing she couldn't be sure. But it was worth it to see the smile on Mr Vincent's face.

'Lovely colours,' he said. 'But it's shapes I like. Look at the shapes of those petals. The way they overlap.'

'Would you like to have a go at sketching them?' Suzie asked. 'I could help you hold the pencil steady. See what we could do, eh?'

'You wouldn't have time to sit and . . .'

'Sure I would,' said Suzie. 'Won't matter if the staff lounge don't get cleaned. Nobody has time to use it anyway.'

She raced upstairs and got a pencil and paper from Jill in reception, without saying what it was for.

'Feels strange,' said Mr Vincent, trying to grip the pencil between his thin fingers. 'I can't do it. It's no good,' he said as the pencil fell onto the tray.

'Don't give up, yet,' said Suzie. 'If I put my hand under your wrist like this . . . give it a bit of support.'

She couldn't help smiling as she placed the pencil back between his fingers. She sounded just like one of her teachers.

'Don't give up just because you can't do it straight away, Suzie.'

Mr Vincent's hand shook as he made a few hesitant marks on the paper.

'Parkinson's disease,' he said, apologetically.

Suzie didn't know what to say. She'd never heard of it. Didn't know the symptoms. Didn't know whether it was likely to get worse. Whether she was really wasting his time. Maybe Matron was right. She should leave well alone. But it bothered her to see them all sitting around, eyes half closed, waiting to die. She glanced round.

'Stay still,' Mr Vincent complained. 'How can I do anything with you squirming about?'

You'd need three, four times the staff to give these people the attention they really needed, Suzie thought. No wonder Matron had been pleading for extra!

Suzie's hand started to ache as time drifted by. She began to think of all the jobs she'd been asked to do, that morning.

'Hey, that's great,' she said as she caught a glimpse of the paper.

'Dreadful,' snarled Mr Vincent, his frail hands suddenly clutching the paper, crumpling, tearing, scattering fragments across the floor.

Suzie was almost crying as she bent to pick them up. She hadn't just been humouring him. She'd meant what she'd said. The flowers really had looked good to her. Easily recognisable as carnations.

She dropped the torn paper into the bin and turned to Mr Vincent. He had slumped down in his chair, head lolling back on the cushions.

'Mr Vincent?' she said.

No answer.

'MR VINCENT!'

One eye opened.

'Are you all right...I thought...'

The other eye opened. She could see the tears, rolling out. Tears of frustration. She knew them well.

'I'm sorry, Mr Vincent. I shouldn't 'ave...'

'I used to be so good,' he said, before his eyes closed again.

Suzie looked at her watch. Almost time to help with the morning break and she hadn't even cleared the breakfast things, let alone cleaned upstairs. She started to wander round, picking up plates and dishes, trying to say a few words to everyone as she hurried past.

'You're just the same as the others,' Bessie muttered.

'What?' said Suzie.

'I was talking to you just then and you never answered.'

'Were you? Didn't I? Sorry. I was thinkin' about all the stuff I've got to do an'...So, what did you want to tell me, then?'

'I was just trying to say thank you, for what you've done.'

'Oh, I haven't done nothing,' said Suzie, looking at Mr Vincent, fast asleep.

At the others, back in their places, where Matron had put them.

'Yes, you have. It's really perked me up, having a lively youngster to talk to. And I choose my own clothes every day now.'

'Well, like you said, Bessie. You're a rebel like me.'

'I was,' said Bessie. 'In my younger days. But it doesn't do.'

'Why not?' said Suzie. 'If you don't stand up for yourself you just get trampled on, don't you?'

'Maybe my problem was that I wasn't rebel enough,' said Bessie. 'When it came to the crunch.'

'What crunch?' said Suzie.

'I was twenty,' said Bessie. 'Not a child, but Mother didn't approve.'

Bessie was clearly lost in the past. Suzie was just lost. She didn't have a clue what Bessie was talking about.

'She said he was too old for me. That he was no good.'

The story was beginning to sound familiar. This could have been Mel talking about Dave.

'Your boyfriend?' said Suzie.

'Fiancé,' said Bessie, proudly. 'We were engaged. At least I thought we were. Otherwise I wouldn't have ... I thought we were going to get married.'

'Why didn't you?' said Suzie, rather more abruptly than she had meant.

'He was already married,' said Bessie. 'I didn't find out until it was too late, of course.'

'Too late?'

Suzie's mind was working overtime. She thought she knew what Bessie meant but it seemed so improbable.

'I was pregnant.'

'Pregnant,' Suzie whispered.

She didn't know why she had whispered. Why she was shocked. She hadn't been shocked last year when her friend Dina had left school to have a kid. It had never bothered her in the slightest that her own parents hadn't been married.

'It was different in those days, you understand,' said Bessie, answering Suzie's unasked questions. 'There was no question of him getting a divorce. Mother was furious. Said I was a disgrace to the family. Packed me off to an aunt so the neighbours wouldn't find out. Even then I wasn't allowed out once it started to show.'

'You're kiddin',' said Suzie.

'Single mothers hadn't really been invented then,' said Bessie wistfully. 'So, of course, there was no question of me keeping the child. I never even thought about it until she was born. I just sort of accepted that she'd have to be adopted. But when I saw her...so tiny...so beautiful, I wanted to keep her. I'd have put up with the stares, the gossip, the disgrace...anything. But my parents wouldn't have it.'

'So what happened?' Suzie breathed.

'They took her away,' said Bessie. 'She was with me three days and then they took her away. That's what I meant, you see. When it came to the crunch I let them take her away.'

Suzie clutched Bessie's hand.

'It weren't your fault. You didn't 'ave no choice, did you? Not in them days. Like you said.'

Bessie shook her head.

'I've only ever told a few people,' she said.

'I'm glad you told me,' said Suzie.

'I know you'll think I'm a stupid old woman,' said Bessie. 'But do you know what? I've never stopped thinking about her in all these years. I used to hope she'd try to trace me ... people do trace their natural families, don't they?'

'I did,' said Suzie. 'A few years after Mum died, Mel, that's my foster mum, helped me trace my dad.'

'I'm sorry ... I didn't know your mother had ...'

'Yeah, well, these things 'appen.'

'And your father ... did you find him?'

'Sort of,' said Suzie. 'I found his family. His parents an' his sisters. I see 'em sometimes but they aren't much interested in me. Don't suppose he would 'ave been neither. I'll never know. Got 'imself killed in a car accident, didn't he? Not long after 'im an' Mum split up. Nobody bothered to tell 'er as far as I know.'

'It doesn't always work out, does it?' said Bessie, almost to herself.

'No but it shouldn't stop you from tryin' if you want to,' said Suzie. 'I was glad I tried 'cos at least I know now, see? I don't 'ave to wonder no more whether he's out there somewhere, thinkin' about me. So you know what I reckon?'

Bessie didn't answer, so Suzie continued.

'I reckon you shouldn't just keep waiting for your

50

daughter to turn up. You should make the first move. Try to trace her.'

The words all came tumbling out before Suzie had a chance to remember Mel's advice and put her brain into gear first. What was she thinking of? Encouraging Bessie to trace a daughter who'd be... er... in her fifties. Who might not be enthusiastic about a blind, frail old woman claiming to be her mother. There were a million ways it could all end in disappointment and only a very slim chance indeed of a happy reunion.

'I couldn't,' said Bessie. 'I wouldn't know how. Not stuck in here.'

There it was. The chance to shrug it off. Forget it as a madcap idea of the moment.

'I know how. I can get it goin'...'

There it went again. Her mouth. Operating without any help from her brain.

'Would you, Suzie...? It would mean such a lot. I wouldn't want to mess up her life. I wouldn't even need to see her. It would be enough just to know... to know if she was happy.'

Suzie couldn't wait to tell Mel when she got home. In fact her head was so full of Bessie and her baby, that she almost bumped into the man loitering outside the Manor. The bald man, who looked quite sinister when you got close up to him. He opened his mouth as if to speak but Suzie hurried past. Perhaps she ought to report it? Stranger danger and all that. There were some right nutters about these days. There'd been a case in the local paper recently about an old woman who'd been assaulted in the park. Suzie shivered. There was crime and crime. Things like that just didn't bear thinking about.

'Mrs Dolby's been on the phone, Suzie,' were Mel's opening words when she got back. 'Says Matron has been onto her complaining about you. She asked me to have a word.'

'Go on then,' said Suzie. 'Have your word. What's the old cow moanin' about now?'

Matron hadn't missed anything out. She'd even made up a few things of her own. The jobs Suzie hadn't got round to doing. How Mr Vincent had been crying and asking for pencils. How the carnations had set off Elsie's chest. How Bessie was over excited, rambling about something Suzie was going to do for her.

'Over excited!' Suzie almost spat out the words. 'Matron thinks they're over excited if they blink. They're allowed to stay alive as long as they're prepared to be vegetables. But they're not vegetables. They're people. Let me tell you about Bessie, Mel.'

By the time she had finished Mel was shaking her head.

'You're right. I could help. I've got enough contacts in social services but Matron would never approve... Language, Suzie!' she snapped as Suzie launched into a colourful description of what she thought of Matron.

'Anyway,' said Suzie, 'we're not talkin' about Matron. We're talkin' about Bessie. Now are you gonna help or what?'

'I don't know... I'll have to think...'

'Think then,' said Suzie. 'I'm going out.'

Mel shook her head as she heard the door slam. She knew what out meant. Hanging around the park or town centre with Dave and her other feckless friends. Getting home late, breath smelling of drink and cigarettes. Attempts at reason turning into rows. Sanctions leading to sulks.

As it happened, her fears on this particular Thursday night were unfounded. Suzie was back early, silent and morose. Which, in a way, was even more worrying.

Chapter 7

Suzie arrived at the Manor the next day in fine mood. Okay, so last night had been a disaster. But Dave would phone tonight. They'd make up. They always did. And besides, she had too much on her mind to worry about Dave.

If Suzie had stopped to think about it, she'd have known how strange that was. For the past six months, long before she ever started going out with him, thoughts of Dave had filled every waking moment and most of her sleeping ones too. Now, all she could think about was the fact that it was Friday. She'd lasted a whole week and what's more, Mel had said she'd help Bessie.

'I'm not promising anything, mind,' Mel had added.

Mel always said that. She was used to covering her tracks. Refusing to raise hopes in kids who'd been let down too many times before. But Mel's maybes, Suzie knew, were better than anyone else's promises.

Suzie lifted her face to the sky. Was it actually bluer today? Was the sun brighter, warmer? Or was it just because she felt good?

She did feel good. It took her a few minutes to recognise the symptoms. It had been a long time since she'd felt this way. But it was definitely sunnier too. It was going to be what the newspapers called a scorcher. Not that it would make any difference to Bessie and the others. Stuck in that rotten basement.

What had Mr Forest said about re-surfacing the car park? She stopped and stared around. The car park was massive. Far too big. It took up a full side of the Manor. The sunny side. What they should do was make it smaller. Use the space to make a little garden. So the old people could sit out. Maybe she should mention it ... and about the man. He'd been there again. Watched her, watching him, before slowly driving away. Creepy!

As it happened she didn't have time to mention anything to anyone in the course of the morning. Everyone seemed determined she should make up for the jobs she hadn't done yesterday. By two o'clock she could barely keep her eyes open. Even with the few windows open, the heat in the basement was stifling.

'I reckon we should get a few of 'em outside before they keel over,' she said to Trish.

'A few of who?'

'You know, Bessie, Mr Vincent ... some of the more active ...'

'The residents! Outside?' said Trish, as if Suzie had suggested a camel trek across the Sahara.

'Yeah, why not? Do 'em good.'

'Can't,' said Trish. 'Nowhere to go.'

'What about that paved courtyard thing?'

'In front of Matron's office?' said Trish. 'No way!'

'Why not? No one's usin' it. Matron's not even in her office. She's gone to a meetin'.'

'Okay, so how do you intend to get them out there?'

'Up in the lifts.'

'Fine.'

'Out the back...'

'Can't. There's steps there and no ramp.'

'Through Matron's office.'

Trish burst out laughing.

'You're a gem, you are! I keep telling my boyfriend what a laugh it's been since you came.'

Suzie looked momentarily hurt and then her face went red. At school, a teacher, seeing that change, would have sent for reinforcements immediately.

'I'm not tryin' to be bloody funny,' she yelled. 'I mean it. It won't do no harm. Now go an' get Annie an' Pat to give us a hand.'

Trish scurried off, glad to be out of the way. By the time she returned with Annie and Pat, all determined to put an end to this madness, Suzie had already pushed two wheelchairs into the lift.

'This is lovely this is,' said Elsie. 'Suzie's taking us out.'

'Can I take a pencil?' said Mr Vincent.

'Don't forget my tablets,' said Lily. 'In case my feet swell up.'

Swollen feet, Suzie found, were just one of the problems of taking old people to sit in a courtyard. It wasn't, as Trish had hinted, as simple as it sounded. There were hats to be found. Sun cream to smear on. Cold drinks to provide. Sunshades to fix into the small round tables. It took forever!

Still, it was worth it once everyone was settled.

'We ought to scatter a bit of sand around, to make it like the beach,' said Suzie.

'Don't push it,' said Trish.

'Here a minute, Suzie,' Mr Vincent called.

She wandered over. Even in this heat some of them had blankets draped over their knees.

'I've got something to show you,' said Mr Vincent delving beneath his blanket. 'I've found a way of doing it.'

He produced a small wooden box, followed by a pencil and some folded bits of paper.

Suzie waited to see what else he might conjure up, but that, it seemed, was it.

'If I rest my wrist on this box, you see, I can steady my hand. Not for long. Ten minutes is the most I can manage at a time but it's a start.'

He started to unravel a piece of paper. Suzie peered down to see if he had improved on his carnations. But it was not flowers she saw. It was ... it was ...

'Brill!' she yelled. 'Trish ...'

She could barely speak for laughing but Trish had got the message. She came over and within seconds she was laughing too.

'Pat ... Annie ...'

From Pat and Annie, the paper passed to the residents. Suzie even tried to describe it to Bessie, feeling, for the first time, what a loss sight must be. Without it you could feel the warmth, smell the flowers, hear the birds but you could never appreciate what Mr Vincent had drawn.

The merriment was so infectious that nobody noticed the impending storm. The two figures breezing through

Matron's office, hovering at the patio doors like dark clouds.

'Don't tell me!' Matron's thunderous voice bellowed. 'This is one of Suzie's good ideas.'

'It wasn't only Suzie,' said Trish bravely facing Matron and Mrs Dolby.

'Hi,' said Suzie, to Mrs Dolby. 'I'd forgotten about your visit.'

'Obviously,' said Matron. 'You've been too busy ransacking my office to think about the trivial matter of a visit from your teacher.'

'But we didn't ...'

'You've moved all my furniture.'

'We had to, to get the wheelchairs through. We were gonna put it back ...'

'And I suppose you were going to clean the carpet too.'

'It's only a few marks.'

Lily Smith started to giggle.

'What's that sil ... Smith woman doing,' said Matron, bearing down on her and snatching a piece of paper from her hand.

Matron stared at the paper and swung to face Suzie.

'Did you do this?'

'You kiddin'?' said Suzie. 'I couldn't do nothin' like that!'

'It's disgraceful,' said Matron. 'Obscene ... it's ... Who is responsible?'

'It's brill,' said Suzie. 'Can't you see ... ?'

Matron clearly couldn't. But Mrs Dolby, who had

peered over her shoulder, could. She smiled at Suzie and winked.

'Mr Vincent did it,' said Suzie. 'And don't go yellin' at him.'

'I won't,' said Matron. 'Because it isn't true. Look at his hands! How could he ... ?'

'I use my box,' said Mr Vincent, holding it up.

Matron glared from him to Suzie and back again.

'He were a cartoonist, see,' said Suzie. 'They're not meant to be real portraits or nothing. You see, he takes your eyes which sort of bulge out a bit and makes 'em even bigger ... '

'I know what a cartoonist does,' Matron snapped. 'I just object to being ridiculed in this way.'

'It's only a bit of fun,' said Suzie, looking at the picture again. At the creature Mr Vincent had drawn. A sort of giant, mutant slug with Matron's features. 'You can easy see who it's supposed to be ... '

'Suzie,' Mrs Dolby warned, quietly. 'When in a hole, stop digging.'

Suzie had stopped listening. Her attention was on Mr Tyler who was nodding, as always, and stretching out his hands.

'You want a drink?' she said.

He nodded. She tried to give him a drink but he pushed it away.

'A tissue?'

He nodded again, before refusing the tissue.

'This could take all day, Mr Tyler,' she said good-humouredly. 'Your hat? Right!'

59

Putting his hat on his head was a tricky business with him nodding all the time. Only when she had finished did she realise Mrs Dolby was close beside her, staring. Staring at Mr Tyler.

It came to Suzie in an instant. She knew she had recognised the name. Had seen it written somewhere. And now she knew where. All those boring assemblies when she had sat in the school hall staring into space. Her glazed eyes had sought distraction in all manner of unlikely places. She had read the names of the netball team, read the anti drugs posters, the pathetic poems written by the clever boys and girls and, when all else failed, the wooden plaque with the names of all the old head teachers on it. And one of them had been Edward Tyler.

'You know 'im, don't you?' Suzie said.

It was Mrs Dolby's turn to nod.

'He was the head when I first started teaching, over thirty years ago. Retired soon after I arrived but I remember him. He was a wonderful teacher.'

Wonderful and teacher were two words Suzie had never imagined could be used in the same sentence. But after Mrs Dolby had raved on for another five minutes, Suzie had got the message. It was hard to imagine that a man who had once managed hundreds of pupils and dozens of staff could be reduced to this. Nodding Ned! What had happened to all that intelligence? Firmness? Personality? How did it feel to a man like that to be treated like an imbecile? Did he know? Did he care?

Mrs Dolby's eyes had misted over, clearly troubled by the same questions.

'There's someone to see you, Mr Tyler,' Suzie suddenly announced. 'Mrs Dol...'

'Miss Harris, I was then...but I don't suppose you remember...'

Mr Tyler nodded. Again and again. His nods becoming more frequent until Suzie feared his head might drop right off.

'Now, Ned,' said Matron. 'Don't go getting excited. Trish, get his tablets.'

'You see,' said Suzie to Mrs Dolby. 'You see what it's like here. Keep 'em doped up so they don't cause any bother. Finish off any poor bloody spark of life they might have left. Dump 'em in that bloody basement like a bunch of flamin' Egyptian mummies.'

Mrs Dolby was too busy being impressed by Suzie's knowledge of Egyptian mummies to notice her language, which was, by Suzie's standards, mild anyway. Matron was another matter.

'We don't have swearing at the Manor.'

'Don't we?' said Suzie. 'Then we can add it to the bloody list, can't we? We don't have fun. We don't have conversations. We don't have bloody lives...'

'Out!' screamed Matron. 'Out and don't come back. Not you or anyone else from your school.'

'Don't worry, I'm goin',' said Suzie. 'At least when I've said goodbye to...'

'You're not saying anything to anybody. You can just...'

'Shut up!'

'What? How dare you! How dare you speak to me

like that!'

Suzie didn't answer. She had dropped on her knees in front of Mr Tyler's wheelchair. Mrs Dolby hovered next to her.

'He said something,' Suzie whispered.

'Don't try to distract attention from your appalling behaviour,' Matron said.

'He said somethin', I tell you! Go on, Mr Tyler. Tell us. Tell us what you said.'

He nodded. Slowly this time. And as he did his lips moved, forcing out what was barely a whisper.

'Good.'

'Good?' Suzie whispered back, failing to see what could possibly be good about the situation.

'Goodbye, pet.'

Chapter 8

Suzie dropped the pen onto the floor and flopped onto her bed, exhausted. It was nearly midday and she still hadn't dressed. She'd barely slept at all last night. She'd sat up till gone midnight talking to Mel and Eric and even then she hadn't been tired.

They'd been very understanding. Sympathetic. Even Mrs Dolby had phoned and put in a good word. Said Suzie had tried. That she had a rapport, whatever that was, with the old people.

Not that it mattered. There was no way Matron was giving her another chance. No way she was having her back for the second week. And why? What had she done? Told the truth, that's what.

Suzie hurled a pillow across the room. Then a hairbrush. A shoe. A box of tissues. A mug of cold coffee. A pile of tapes. It didn't help. There weren't enough objects in the room to feed her anger. She didn't answer the knock on her door. Didn't move as it was pushed open. Didn't respond as Mel screamed.

'Suzie! What have you...I heard the noise...and...oh, no!'

Mel ignored the coffee stain spreading across the carpet, the debris on the floor and stared instead at the bedroom walls. Lumps of Blu-tack lurked where posters had been ripped off to make way for obscene words, scrawled in thick, red felt tip.

Mel picked up the offending pen from where Suzie had dropped it. She hadn't seen this sort of carnage for at least twelve months. Not since the day Suzie found out that the dad she'd never known was dead.

'Suzie,' Mel repeated, more quietly.

'So?'

If there had been any sign of repentance, Mel would have acted differently. As it was, she faced Suzie's challenge.

'So,' she said. 'You'll have to clear it up. Two or three coats of paint might cover the felt tip. In the meantime please keep your door closed. I don't want the little ones reading that lot. And by the way,' she said, pointing to one of the words. 'It's two gs in the middle.'

'It's not fair,' Suzie screamed at her.

'I think it's very fair,' said Mel. 'You know the rules. You make the mess. You clear it up.'

'Not that,' said Suzie, swinging her legs over the side of the bed. 'The Manor. I didn't do nothing.'

Mel sighed and sat on the edge of the bed next to Suzie. They had been through it all last night. Suzie had seemed to understand. To grasp that she had, in part, been responsible. That she shouldn't have sworn at Matron. Shouldn't have questioned the Manor's competence quite so brutally. Should have exercised a bit more self control. And now this! All pretence of control thrown away along with the pillow and the coffee mug. All the improvements of the past year, vanished.

Improvements! Suzie hadn't exactly been a saint but

64

she had settled a bit. Learnt to talk without shouting. To get along with the other children. To cope with minor problems and disappointments in a rational way.

This, then, was obviously no minor disappointment. The Manor, the old people, clearly meant more to Suzie than even Mel had imagined. And there was nothing she could do. No help she could offer. Last night Eric had talked to Suzie about going to college. Taking a course as a carer but she had shrugged it off.

'Nah. I'd 'ave to do writin' an' stuff. I'd never stick at it. Besides, I aren't gonna pass any G.C.S.E.s and they don't let you in without a few of them.'

'Mrs Dolby said you could,' Eric had persisted. 'If you went to her lunchtime help sessions.'

'For thickos.'

'For people who need a bit of extra help.'

'Nah. It wouldn't do no good.'

They had dropped the subject. Decided to wait until Suzie was in a more receptive mood. No point raising it again now when Suzie's level of self confidence had dropped right off the scale. But what to do? What to say to someone who had failed at possibly the only thing she had ever wanted to do in her life before.

It was Suzie, surprisingly, who offered an answer.

'You're mad at me, aren't you?'

Mel repeated the words she had said so many times before.

'I'm not pleased with what you've done, Suzie. And, yes, you could say I'm a bit mad at you but I still love you.'

'So you'll still do it?'

'Do what?'

'Help me to help Bessie? I promised, you see. An' I got the stuff from her yesterday mornin',' she said, producing a crumpled piece of paper out of her bag. 'You know. The stuff you asked me to get about where she lived and where her auntie lived and that.'

Mel nodded. At worst, it would lead to yet another major disappointment. At best, a happy reunion. And, if she was lucky, in a week or two, Suzie would forget all about it.

Suzie ran the paint roller across the faint shadow of the f-word. It was quite good fun, painting. On Saturday afternoon, she'd cleaned the stain off the carpet, put down a plastic sheet and gone off to the shops, with Eric, to choose some paint. She'd settled on a darker shade than she'd fancied at first because Eric had said it would only take two coats instead of three or four. He was right. They'd done the first last night. Now the words were disappearing nicely.

Eric had been a big help. She didn't know whether he was being nice or whether he simply didn't trust her to do it on her own.

'It don't cost much, does it?' she said.

'What?'

'Paint.'

She knew that because she'd had to make a contribution out of her pocket money. But then Eric had given her double, because he said she'd tried.

'Not really, why?'

'I was just thinkin' about the residents' lounge. It's a load of rot Mr Forest sayin' they can't afford it. 'Course they could if they wanted to.'

'Careful!' yelled Eric, as Suzie almost fell off the step ladder. 'Don't think and paint at the same time. It's dangerous!'

'Is that the phone?' said Suzie, waving her roller in her excitement.

It might be Dave. Must be Dave. She'd phoned him last night. Left a message with his mum. Told her it was urgent. She needed him. Needed someone who could take her mind off things.

'Keep still,' said Eric. 'Mel's downstairs. She'll get it.'

Suzie put down her roller and waited for Mel to call. But she didn't. Eventually Suzie went back to her painting and barely noticed when Mel sidled in.

'Looks good,' she said. 'Fancy taking a break? That was Matron on the phone. I've got something to tell you.'

Suzie wiped her roller as Eric instructed, though perhaps not so carefully as he would have liked. She was in a hurry. Desperate to know what Matron had to moan about this time. Probably the table Suzie had knocked over in the hall as she stormed out. Or had she discovered the missing magazines which Suzie had borrowed on Wednesday and neglected to take back? She couldn't have them now, anyway. They were in the bin, torn to shreds.

67

Suzie slumped into a chair at the kitchen table, picked up a biscuit and waited as Mel poured some tea.

'I don't quite know how to put this,' said Mel, looking as though she was about to burst out laughing at any minute. 'But they want you back, Suzie. They want you to do your second week.'

Suzie said nothing. She knew it wasn't possible. That Mel had somehow got it wrong. There was no way Matron would have changed her mind.

'Apparently,' Mel went on, 'the residents have got up a petition.'

'A pet what?' said Suzie.

'You know,' said Mel. 'A list of names. Saying they want you back.'

'Come off it,' said Suzie. 'Matron wouldn't take no notice of that if they'd signed with their own blood.'

'She might. She wouldn't want them getting all worked up. But the crucial factor is that it's the weekend.'

'So?'

'That's when most of them have their visitors. Your friend Bessie started it off. Telling her ex-neighbour. Then she spread the word to Lily Smith's grandson, home from university. Matron doesn't approve of Lily's grandson. He's into Greenpeace and animal rights. The petition was his idea.'

'This is amazing,' said Eric.

'Outrageous, was the word Matron used. Anyway, Justin, that's the grandson, took the petition home on Saturday and got all the family to sign it. This morning,

Elsie's visitors signed up and Harry's and Barbara's and...oh, I forget all the names. Matron was still wavering, I think, when Mr Vincent, who hasn't got any family to back him, said he was going on hunger strike.'

'Hunger strike!' said Eric, spilling his tea onto the table.

'Nothing short of revolution, Matron called it,' Mel said. 'I had to bite my lip to stop myself laughing.'

'Well, Suzie,' said Eric. 'It seems you've started the strangest revolution in history. What are you going to do about it?'

'Uh?' said Suzie, who was never quite sure whether Eric was teasing or not.

'I suggest you go back on Monday before it spreads,' he said. 'You never know. They might form a union. Blockade the high street with their wheelchairs. Hold Matron hostage.'

'It's not funny,' Suzie snapped.

'No, it's not,' Eric agreed. 'It's marvellous. It's a great tribute to you, Suzie.'

Suzie wasn't sure what a tribute was but she knew this was praise and hung her head to hide her blushes.

'On the other hand,' Eric continued, 'you shouldn't take it as a sign that you can do as you like. These old people have gone to a lot of trouble for you. Don't let them down. Get on with the work. Be polite and absolutely no more swearing at Matron.'

Suzie nodded. She was so happy that, right at that moment, she would have agreed to anything. Eric picked up the message.

'Shall we finish that painting then?'

The first thing Suzie planned to do on Monday morning was to tell Matron about the strange man. He'd been there again, driving off when he saw Suzie watching him. But she didn't get a chance. Matron was obviously avoiding her and had spent most of the morning shut in her office with Dr Grenville. Annie and Pat barely spoke. Suzie thought they were just cross. Trish said it was because they were jealous. Couldn't understand what the residents liked about her, Trish said. But she could.

'You're like a breath of fresh air in this place, Suzie. I wish I had your guts.'

'I wish I had your brains,' said Suzie. 'Tell me about that college course you had to do.'

They worked as they talked. Every now and again, Suzie caught Trish looking at her strangely, as if she was waiting for her to say or do something.

'Anything wrong?' Suzie asked, eventually.

'No. You're all right, are you?'

'Yeah. Why?'

'Nothing. I just thought . . . you might have been . . . a bit . . . er . . . upset.'

'Nah. I'm fine,' said Suzie, thinking about the mess she'd made of her room. 'Now.'

They'd been doing the bedrooms, so Suzie didn't see her old friends until mid morning when she and Trish served the snacks. The atmosphere in the basement surprised her. Sure, they were pleased to see her but they were quieter than she'd expected. Maybe their little revolution had tired them out. She'd have to be careful. No more stirring things. No more excitement.

'Where's Mr Tyler?' she suddenly asked Trish. 'I've saved him a macaroon. He likes macaroons.'

Lily groaned. Elsie started to cough.

'You don't know?' said Trish, patting Elsie's back. 'Matron hasn't told you. That's why you're so ...'

'Hasn't told me what?' Suzie said, as Trish grabbed her arm and dragged her towards the kitchen.

'Sit down,' she said, waving at Annie to go and take over in the lounge.

Trish looked at Suzie. There was no easy way to do this. She remembered her own first time. And the next and the next. What she couldn't remember was when she had started to get used to it. When it had stopped hurting. Maybe she hadn't. Maybe it still did. But the first time was the worst.

'I'm afraid Mr Tyler passed away,' said Trish. 'Late last night. In his sleep. The night staff found him when they did the last check.'

Suzie sat silently for a moment, letting the images drift across her mind. The popular headmaster telling his funny stories in assemblies. The old man quietly nodding away his last five years. The body, lying in a dark room, all alone, head finally still. Another body. Another room. Another death.

She leapt up as the pain split her temples. Stillness and silence no longer possible, she prepared for action.

71

Chapter 9

Suzie didn't know how she managed to get through the rest of the day. No, that wasn't true. She knew exactly how she'd done it. By blocking it out. Like she did with everything that made her unhappy.

First, while the bemused Trish had waited for tears, Suzie had picked up a mop and started attacking the kitchen floor until it gleamed like a sheet of ice.

'Girl's trying to kill us now,' Pat had complained as she skidded towards the sink.

Suzie had wiped, sprayed, shaken, polished everything that could be wiped, sprayed, shaken or polished. And even a few things that couldn't.

'She'll be at Harry's bald head with that duster in a minute,' Annie had moaned.

All the time she had chatted. To Lily about her grandson, Justin. To Elsie about her chest. To Bessie about Mel's plans to start the search. To Mr Vincent about his latest sketch. At any other time his cartoon of Dr Grenville and Mr Forest as a pair of skeletons would have made her laugh. But not today.

Today was not a day for laughing. It was a day for being angry. Angry that Mr Tyler had died and that nobody had bothered to tell her. As if it didn't matter! It was a day for stamping and swearing, as Mel had found out.

Mel hadn't attempted to stop her. She had simply

ushered her into the kitchen, away from the other children, and watched her spill out the aggression she had bottled up all day at the Manor.

And now. Now it was gone midnight. Suzie lay on her bed, lights full on, scared of the thoughts which came in the dark. The hurt that surfaced when the anger died. When you were alone. When you couldn't block it out any more.

Even the lights weren't helping much tonight. They couldn't reach the really dark places. The ones in your mind. The deep, bubbling pits of fear and thoughts of death.

'Goodbye, pet,' Edward Tyler had said.

Had he known? Was it coincidence that the last and only words he had said in five years were so definite? So final? And why did she care? He was an old man. She'd only known him a week. Was the hurt she felt strong enough on its own or was it stirring up other things? Other, long buried pain?

'It was a blessing, really,' Trish had tried to tell her. 'It was no life for him, was it? Sitting there, nodding to himself, day after day. Ninety is a good innings.'

'Better than twenty-six,' Suzie had muttered, but Trish had not understood.

Not understood that it was no life for Suzie's mother either. The tiny flat with the boarded-up windows. No point repairing 'em, they just got broke again. As easily broken as arms or jaws when Des got mad. Or was it Paul? Maybe Wayne. He was always lurking around somewhere. He was the one she depended on. He supplied the stuff. He controlled the highs and lows. Mostly lows in the end. Crouching on the mud brown carpet throwing up. Barely able to stand without shaking. Falling into deep sleeps for hours on end. No life.

Was she like poor Mr Tyler? Better off dead?

'No!'

Suzie screamed the word aloud. She had no right. No right to die like that. To leave her.

'It weren't like that, Suzie. I never meant to do it.'

Suzie blinked. Stared. Blinked again. It didn't make any difference. There was someone standing by the end of the bed. Someone she hadn't seen in a long time.

'Mum?'

'It were an accident, Suzie. I loved yer, yer know. I wouldn't have left yer.'

Suzie stretched out her hand and pulled it away again. This was crazy. It couldn't be real. It was a dream for sure. Like the others. The dreams where she saw her mum. Spoke to her. Held her. Dreams that were so real, she woke up truly believing her mum was still alive. But only for a moment. The warm happiness always gave way to the chill of disappointment as tears cascaded onto a bed in someone else's home.

Suzie sat up. Blinked. Rubbed her eyes. Willing the image to go. Before she got sucked in. Started to believe her mother was really there.

'I miss you, Suzie.'

No doubt now. She was fully awake. This was no dream. But if not a dream then . . . Suzie smiled. Ghosts were supposed to be frightening. But they weren't. Not when you knew them. Knew they'd never harm you. She stretched out her arms.

'I miss you too, Mum.'

She was talking to an empty room. Her mother had vanished as suddenly as she had appeared. As if the words had broken a spell.

'Mum!' Suzie screamed. 'Come back. Don't go. Don't leave me.'

'Suzie. SUZIE!'

Mel shook Suzie's shoulders, trying to get a response from the green eyes, open, yet unseeing. Slowly the eyes started to focus. Mel recognised the disappointment just as she had recognised the words. The words eight-year-old Suzie had been screaming when they took her mother's body away. The words she always cried out in her sleep.

'She was here,' Suzie said, flopping back on the pillow.

Mel squeezed her hand.

'It's hardly surprising,' Mel said, gently, 'that the dream came back, with Mr Tyler dying and ... '

'It weren't a dream,' said Suzie firmly.

'All right.'

'You don't believe me.'

'It doesn't matter what I believe.'

'It's true. I saw her. I reckon if you love someone enough you can always see 'em. An' I did love 'er, you know.'

'Of course you did,' said Mel. 'She was your mum.'

'You understand, don't you?' said Suzie, unexpectedly. 'You're not just sayin' it. You really do understand. Other families I stayed with, they couldn't get it, see? They thought that 'cos my mum was on drugs,'cos she left me on my own a lot, 'cos she didn't look after me proper, I couldn't have loved her. But love's not about nice things and regular meals, is it? 'Cos if it was I would have loved all them foster parents. I'd love y...'

She stopped. Mel pretended she hadn't noticed. Tried not to betray the feeling of hopelessness that came over her at times like this. Suzie hadn't told her anything new. There was no way Suzie would ever love her or Eric. Maybe she'd never love anybody in her life again. And, whatever she tried to do for Suzie, whatever kinds of comfort she'd tried to offer, she would only ever touch the surface.

She sat, holding Suzie's hand, until she drifted off to sleep again.

A troubled sleep, Mel could see, the following morning. Suzie, barely awake, groped her way around the house and slouched off, with not a word. If it was a school day, Mel would have bet on her never arriving. At least, this morning, she could be fairly confident she was heading for the Manor.

'You've been crying,' Bessie said.

'How d'you know?' said Suzie.

It was true. As soon as she'd seen the Manor she'd burst into tears, right there in the car park, with the bald man staring. Must definitely remember to mention him

76

to Matron, today! But she'd splashed her face on arrival. Wiped away the telltale signs, which Bessie couldn't have seen anyway.

'I can hear it in your voice.'

'I had a bad night,' said Suzie.

She would have gone on to explain but Annie called her.

'Take Mrs S – I mean Lily, to the lounge, will you?'

'But she's here already,' said Suzie.

'Not the residents' lounge,' Annie snapped. 'Upstairs. The staff lounge! She's got a visitor. That grandson of hers.'

So that's how they did it, Suzie thought, as she wheeled Lily towards the lift. Visitors in the staff lounge! Bet they never got to see downstairs or the poky bedrooms unless they had to.

Lily was dressed in a navy skirt with matching top. Hardly the height of fashion but decent enough. Was this because of her visitor or had Bessie roped her into the campaign? Suzie was still thinking about this as she pushed Lily into the lounge where Justin was waiting.

Suzie wasn't sure of the procedure. Did she just shove the wheelchair in and leave? Was she expected to make a bit of polite conversation? Offer them tea? After Friday's episode she decided against using her own initiative. She would nip straight out and ask Trish about refreshments.

Her plan, simple as it was, was shattered when she made the mistake of looking at Justin who was looking at her. He was talking to his gran but most definitely staring at Suzie. She knew, for a moment, what rabbits must feel when caught in the glare of advancing headlights. And the experience wasn't pleasant.

Justin's eyes were as unremarkable as his face. As his hair. As his clothes. He was not how Suzie had imagined a student to look. Especially one who was into Greenpeace, animal rights and organising petitions for little old ladies. He didn't look at all like the revolutionary Matron had described.

But the unremarkable brown eyes told her one thing. If he was not what she had imagined, then she was certainly not what he expected. They scanned, assessed and almost rolled in disbelief before Justin abandoned his gran and moved towards her.

'You're Suzie?'

'Yeah.'

'Justin.'

'I know.'

'Of course.'

'I'll be off then.'

She said the words but stayed, rooted to the spot. Like waiting to be dismissed from the head's office.

'Something wrong?' she said, as he continued to stare.

'No. Er... nothing. It's just that... Gran's told me so much about you. Everybody did... at the weekend...'

'Lovely girl,' Lily chipped in.

Suzie could almost hear the words scrape across Justin's brain, like nails across a blackboard. She was not, she knew, his idea of a lovely girl. She tried to picture what he was seeing. The studs. The cropped hair, in what the school described as an unnatural colour. The clothes that she'd chosen with Dave and which Mel had scowled at.

'Clothes give out messages,' Mel had said.

No doubt about the message Justin was receiving. A message that the old people didn't seem to get at all. For the first time, she realised that not one of them had questioned her appearance. Not her clothes nor the aggressive frown she knew creased her forehead, even when she smiled.

Bessie had an excuse, of course. But the others? Were they really so short sighted? So vacant? So disinterested? Or was it something else? Did age give you the experience to look below the surface? And even if it did, didn't they know that what was inside Suzie Lawrence was even worse than the bits that showed? Stupid. Senile, the lot of them. That was the only explanation.

'Eh?'

She realised that Justin had been speaking and that she hadn't heard a word he'd said. Thick as well as ugly. Not that she cared what he thought. Why should she? She didn't care what anyone thought, least of all a prat in a polo shirt and designer jeans.

'I said you've really livened the place up. I don't know what you've done, exactly, but I've noticed a change in Gran, this holiday.'

'Have you?'

'She's been talking a lot more. Usually we talk about the old days. Before I was born! They tell me her short term memory is going. But she told me a whole lot about you. She had no trouble with that, at all.'

'Yeah. Well. I've gotta go now. Work to do.'

'I might see you tomorrow, then,' Justin said. 'I try to come every day in the holidays. Only chance I get. It's too far to come home at weekends in termtime.'

'What is?'

'University.'

'Oh, yeah. Where you at, then?'

Justin lowered his eyes before answering.

'Blimey!' said Suzie.

Chapter 10

'He's at Oxford and he talks dead posh,' Suzie informed Mel. 'Still, he can't be all bad if he comes to see his gran every day.'

Mel smiled at Suzie's assumption that anyone who was clever was automatically bad news. Thinking of news led her to remember her own which she planned to announce the moment there was a break in Suzie's rather one-sided conversation. These nightly monologues about the Manor had become the norm, making Mel almost wish Suzie was back at school when you could barely drag a sentence out of her.

'He brought Lily some photos which she showed me. And Mr Vincent's done another cartoon. And Elsie's on these new tablets for her bowels...'

'Spare me Elsie's bowels,' Mel groaned, as she stirred the cheese sauce.

'Okay. But Bessie said...'

'Ah, Bessie,' said Mel. 'Perhaps I can get a word in edgeways now.'

'Have you found her? Have you found out?'

'Not quite but we've made some progress. Bessie's daughter was adopted by a family called Lister. They called her Anne. We know where they lived and where they moved to. But then they moved again and we lost the trail.'

'Oh,' said Suzie.

'Don't go all grumpy on me,' said Mel. 'We haven't given up yet. Sherlock Shaw's working on it.'

Suzie smiled. His name wasn't really Sherlock, she knew. They called him that after some detective called Sherlock Holmes 'cos he had a reputation for being able to find people. It was him who'd helped find her dad. Or rather his family.

'Oh, and I had an idea, today,' said Suzie, prompted by the thought of families. 'You know Mr Vincent doesn't have no family? Well, I thought you an' Eric could pop an' visit him sometimes.'

'Did you?' said Mel, thinking how impossible it would be to fit in and how she'd probably end up doing it anyway.

Suzie nodded. She'd had another thought about Mr Vincent too. Something that would have to wait until tomorrow.

On Wednesday a cloud was hovering over Suzie as she walked round the Manor. She could feel it, dark, oppressive, menacing. It took her a while to realise what it was. At first she thought it was because Dave still hadn't phoned. Or the worry about the man in the car park. He'd definitely been giving her funny looks when she passed last night. And she still hadn't got round to telling anyone. But, no, it wasn't either of those. It had only appeared after she had spoken to Mr Vincent.

'I was wonderin',' she'd said, 'if you could do one of them cartoon things. Of me.'

'If you like,' he'd said. 'Only I'll have to get cracking

because you finish on Friday, don't you?'

That was it then. Something else she'd blocked out until Mr Vincent forced it into her mind. Only two more days to go and then it was over. Back to school. No more Bessie and Elsie and Lily to think about. Was that it? Was that what she liked about being at the Manor? It gave her something to think about, other than herself. Took her mind off the dismal past and even more dismal future stretching out in front of her.

'Hi.'

The greeting disturbed her. She turned to see Justin wheeling Lily towards the lift.

'She drifted off to sleep,' he said. 'Must have been my boring conversation!'

'Nah,' said Suzie. 'It's just that she isn't used to so much company. None of 'em are. Usually only get visitors at the weekends, most of 'em. Your gran 'asn't had nobody apart from you since I've been here.'

'Mum comes when she can,' said Justin. 'But she goes away a lot on business. And Dad's got his own accountancy firm. Works all hours. And my brother's wife's just had a baby so . . . '

'You don't have to make excuses for 'em,' said Suzie. 'It aren't none of my business.'

'I wasn't,' said Justin. 'Well, yes I suppose I was, really. It gets me down when they don't bother to come and see her. We don't live far away. We chose this place because it was near.'

'I wondered why people did,' said Suzie. 'Trish says most don't even look round properly. They're so desperate to get their old folks out of the way, they'd settle for anything.'

'I think that's a bit of an exaggeration.'

'Do you?' said Suzie, in the tone she reserved for answering her least favourite teachers.

'Yes. I mean you make it sound like some sort of dumping ground.'

'Isn't it?'

'No. At least, it's a pretty expensive one if it is,' he added, smiling.

'Oh, that's all right then, isn't it?' said Suzie. 'But d'you never think where the money's going? Have you seen Dr Grenville's Jag or Mr Forest's Merc? I have. I notice cars. And they're both brand new!'

'But my gran's well looked after,' he insisted.

'That's what they said to me when I kept running away from care, weren't it? They look after you, don't they, Suzie? You get regular meals and a bed to sleep in. Big bloody deal! What good's that when nobody ever talks to you or takes the trouble to know how you feel?'

If Justin was shocked by these revelations he didn't let it show.

'I'll tell you what,' said Suzie. 'If your gran an' the others could do a bunk, like I did, I reckon they would.'

'Why? I still don't see what's so bad.'

'Come on then,' said Suzie. 'I'll show you.'

Justin's guided tour took a little longer than Suzie expected. She phoned Mel to explain that she'd be staying late that night to catch up on her jobs. No point upsetting Matron again. And besides, she didn't mind staying. She got the polish from the cupboard and headed towards the staff lounge.

Her path was blocked by someone loitering in the doorway. A middle-aged man. The man from the car park. The bald man.

'Can I help you?'

'I was looking for Marie.'

Marie? There weren't any Maries at the Manor. She looked at the man. He was definitely a bit odd. Really creepy and sly looking. A right pervert. Why hadn't she done something? Told someone earlier. Now it was too late. He was right here inside the Manor. Up to goodness knows what.

'Er...we haven't got a Marie...I'll go and check with the office.'

'No need to do that,' he said, taking a step nearer.

Suzie stepped back quickly and screamed as he stretched his hand towards her.

He leapt back, crashing into Annie who had come to see what the fuss was about.

'Suzie! What on earth...?'

'It's him,' said Suzie. 'He's bin hangin' round the place. I reckon he's one of them nutters who...well...I meant to tell someone and now he's...'

'This is Mr Clarke,' said Annie, calmly.

'Mr Clarke?' Suzie repeated.

'Marie's husband,' he said, stretching out his hand again for Suzie to shake.

Even then it took Suzie a couple of seconds to register.

'Oh my goodness,' Annie spluttered. 'She thought you were a ... wait till I tell Pat this one.'

Only when Annie turned and went off giggling down the corridor did the pieces start to fit together.

Mr Clarke. Mrs Clarke. Matron. She had a husband. And a first name. Marie. Knowing that made her suddenly seem a bit more human. Just a bit. And what about him? What must he think?

'I'm sorry,' she said. 'I thought ... what I mean is ... I've seen you lurk ... sitting in the car park ... '

'Marie doesn't drive. I drop her off. Pick her up most nights. She was supposed to be early tonight but I can't find her.'

'Isn't she in her office?'

'No. That's why I started looking round. We're off to our daughter's tonight. Babysitting for our grand-children.'

More surprises. It was hard enough to imagine Matron as a wife, let alone a mother and grandmother!

'What I mean is that I'll be babysitting while Marie falls asleep as usual,' he said. 'I keep telling her she ought to retire or go part-time now. This job's getting too much for her. She works so hard. But there's no point telling her. It's her life, this place. She loves it.'

Suzie tried not to open and close her mouth like a bemused cod. Works hard? Loves it? The man was obviously a nutter after all.

'Of course Marie says I'm being selfish. And she might be right. I had to take early retirement from the police because of my back ... '

The police! Well, that explained why he looked so sneaky. Her instincts about him hadn't been so wrong after all. What would Dave say when she told him she'd been talking to a cop!

'I fill my time all right but it gets a bit lonely,' Mr Clarke said, as though he really was desperate to talk to someone. 'It'd be nice to have company some days. I get a bit low on my own. Having Marie around would cheer me up...Nasty cough you've got,' he said, handing Suzie a tissue as she started to splutter.

She took the tissue, covered her face and tried to pull herself together. It wasn't easy. The thought of Matron actually cheering anybody up was bringing tears to her eyes.

'So how's it going?'

'Uh?' was all Suzie managed to say.

'Work experience. You are Suzie, aren't you?'

'Er...yeah. An' it's okay. I like the old people.'

'And they like you from what I hear.'

Suzie scowled at him. Who did he think he was conning? Anything she said would be written down and used as evidence later, over the babysitting.

'Yeah, well, I'm sure you know all about it. I reckon I'll go an' do the basement now. I'll let Matron know you're here, if I see 'er.'

Matron was, in fact, downstairs, helping the night staff hand out tablets before the residents were taken to their rooms. She accepted the message, nodded curtly and left.

'What are them for?' Suzie asked the night nurse, as

Mr Vincent swallowed two white tablets.

'To control the Parkinson's disease.'

Suzie nodded.

'And what about the yellow one?'

'That's just a vitamin supplement.'

'And that big one?'

'Sleeping pill.'

'An' that capsule thing?'

'Why are you asking so many questions?'

'Just interested. I'm on work experience. I'm supposed to be learnin' somatt, aren't I?'

'Sounds more like snooping than learning to me.'

'Why should I be snooping?'

'I don't know. Pat said she reckoned you might be a plant.'

A plant, Suzie thought. What was the woman on about? Did she look like a geranium?

'You know. Sent in by the health inspectors or some newspaper to check up,' the night nurse explained.

'Don't be thick. They wouldn't send no one like me, would they?'

'Who knows what they'd stoop to after what they've been saying on the news. You must have seen it?'

'Nah, never watch the news. So who's been sayin' what?'

'Do-gooders who think they know everything,' said the nurse, in answer to the first part of the question. 'Saying we use too many drugs in residential homes. Just to keep them quiet.'

'And do you?' said Suzie, looking at the rows of bottles.

'We use what we have to. If patients are likely to get worked up we give them tranquillisers. If they can't sleep we give them sleeping tablets. If they're sick, we treat them. Now, if you've got a problem with that, write to your M.P. and stop pestering me about it.'

Suzie half-heartedly ran her duster over the furniture. Did she have a problem with it? Dead right she did. And it wasn't the only problem either. But what could she do? She was only here for another two days and she'd promised she wouldn't cause bother. On the other hand, could she really leave, having done nothing? Knowing that Bessie and Lily and the others would live and die doped up in that dingy basement?

She turned to take a last look at it, before heading for the lift. Maybe the nurse was right. Maybe she should write to someone. All very well if you knew how to write letters. Which she didn't.

Her thoughts had just turned to someone who did, when she heard raised voices, coming from Matron's office where Mr Clarke had clearly found his wife.

'You're not taking that lot with you?' he was saying.

'When else am I supposed to do it? I don't get time to do paperwork during the day. We're short staffed. And now they're telling me, that instead of getting the extra I asked for, I've got to cut the number of qualified nurses. Savings they want! Do you know how much profit we made last year? And is it enough? Oh no!'

'I don't know why you stick it. You don't have to . . . '

'Oh, no. I don't have to. But what would happen if I left? Who'd try to get Mr Forest to part with his money then?'

'Suzie?' Mr Clarke offered.

Matron laughed. Suzie felt her shoulders tighten, her fists clench.

'If that girl only knew how much I envy her!'

That girl's mouth had dropped open, as she tried to edge back down the corridor before she was discovered.

'Wouldn't it be great to be like that once in a while?' Matron said, laughing again. 'Say what you think. Hang the consequences. I did let her loose on Dr Grenville and Mr Forest once. It didn't do any good, of course, but it was fun to watch...in a way!'

'Don't tell me you're starting to like the girl, after everything you've said.'

'I don't think I dislike her,' said Matron. 'I mean she's as thick as a plank and has absolutely no idea of how to go about things. She's rude, aggressive, subtle as the proverbial sledge-hammer and more likely to make things worse rather than better. But, funnily enough, beneath that ghastly exterior, she does actually care. And, no, I don't dislike her. I suppose, if anything, I feel sorry for her. She hasn't got a hope! Girls like that don't stand a chance, do they?'

Chapter 11

'Patronising cow! Who does she think she is? Feels sorry for me! Doesn't stand a chance! Ghastly, she said I was.'

'Told yer,' said Gemma. 'Work experience is crap.'

Lisa nodded sympathetically. The three boys carried on talking about the previous night's football.

Suzie kicked the park fence and threw her empty can of lager across the grass.

'Can't believe yer've stuck it so long,' said Lisa. 'Yer quite a stranger.'

It was true. Since starting at the Manor, Suzie had been too tired to go out at night. Then, at the weekend, she'd had her room to do. So she'd only seen her mates twice in the whole fortnight. Once last week and now tonight. Last week had been a disaster. Dave had said she'd become a right boring bitch with her little old ladies and poor old men who couldn't draw proper no more. Said they ought to put the whole bloody lot of them to sleep, like they do with animals. Spend the money they saved on pensions on putting up dole money for people like him who couldn't get a job. Build some decent clubs for teenagers, Lisa had said. In the end, they'd all sided with Dave and Suzie had walked off.

She'd expected Dave to phone but he hadn't. So she'd wandered down to the park on the off chance of meeting up with him. Now he was ignoring her. She didn't blame him really. Perhaps she had become a bore. She hadn't meant to talk about the Manor tonight but somehow she couldn't help it.

'Cheer up, Suze,' Gemma was saying. 'Yer can come round our house termorra.'

'What d'yer mean?'

'Well there's no point goin' back ter school fer two days is there?'

Suzie said nothing.

'Yer surely not goin' ter the Manor after what she said about yer?' Lisa screeched.

'It don't really matter what Matron says,' said Suzie shrugging. 'It's the old...'

A string of expletives cut across their conversation.

Dave had given up on football and turned to face her.

'Yer've gone barmy, you 'ave,' he sneered. 'I reckon it must be catchin'. This dementia or whatever they call it.'

'Yeah, I reckon,' said Suzie, trying to smile, trying to lighten the tone.

'I mean if yer'd really rather spend yer time with a bunch of loonies peeing and shitting all over the place, just say so. I mean we won't be offended will we, Gem?' said Dave.

'D'yer 'ave to?' said Gemma. 'It makes me feel sick.'

'It don't make Suzie sick, does it?'

'No, it doesn't,' said Suzie. 'Someone has to look after them. Their families don't want 'em.'

'Someone has ter look after them,' Dave mocked. 'Saint bloody Suzie. Don't sound right somehow.'

Suzie laughed. No point getting into a row again.

She'd come out to try and make it up. Dave was okay really. Good fun and drop dead gorgeous. They'd been going out for two months now. Ever since he'd split up from Dina. He said she'd become a real miserable cow since she'd had the kid. No time for him except when she was after maintenance. Bleating on about the price of nappies and second-hand push chairs. What a bore! Well, Dina's loss was Suzie's gain and she wasn't about to make the same mistake. Dave got bored easily.

Change the subject. Change the subject, Suzie told herself. But all she could think of was poor Mr Tyler, Bessie's search and Lily Smith's grandson. That was definitely a no-go area. She couldn't tell Dave about Justin.

'I think it's time fer a bit of action,' said Dave, nudging the other two lads.

They looked across the park. An elderly woman and her small dog were coming towards them. She had a lead in one hand and a handbag in the other.

Suzie stared at Dave. This was a wind-up. To pay her back for going on about her old people. He wasn't really going to do anything. It was still light for a start. The woman had a dog. Okay, hardly a Rottweiler. One of them stupid little terrier things. But it might bark. The park was patrolled by a keeper on a motor cycle. He could turn up any minute.

While Suzie rattled off endless reasons why Dave wasn't serious, the boys and Gernma had started to amble forward. Lisa leant against the fence. She wasn't a one for getting involved but she was the best look-out in the business. She could spot a store detective at twenty paces. Would keep a shopkeeper talking for ages while one of her mates helped themselves.

Saint Suzie. No it didn't sound right. She'd done her fair share of stuff with the rest but never anything like this. She didn't think Dave had either. But she didn't know. Not for sure. He always seemed to have plenty of money. For someone who'd never worked.

Before she could stop herself, she'd followed him. Gripped his arm.

'She won't 'ave nowt. Nobody carries money round the park no more.'

'Wrinklies do,' said Dave. 'Stupid, see? They think it's safer than leavin' it at home.'

'They've got the patrol now.'

'Scared, are yer?'

'No. I aren't scared. I just aren't gonna let yer do it, that's all.'

There it was. Out. No pretences. No excuses. That could be Elsie out there. Or Lily. And she wasn't going to stand by and watch them get...

HURT. The pain ripped across her face before she realised what had happened. Before she saw Dave's fist raised again and smashing into her cheek bone. The other boys froze. Gemma ran back towards Lisa. This time his foot lashed out. No one was going to...

'STOP that.'

The hoarse voice surprised him. Made him stop long enough for Suzie to put some distance between them. To realise that it was the old woman who had shouted. The old woman who was now just a few paces away.

'Shut it, yer interferin' old bitch!' Dave growled as the woman started to yell at him and the dog began to bark. 'Come on, Suze,' he pleaded. 'I didn't mean it. I lost it fer a minute, that's all. Grab the bag, Suze.'

The old woman winced at Suzie's two word response. Cringed as Dave lurched forward and snatched the bag. Stood helpless and bemused as Suzie lashed out, kicking his shins, ripping the bag from his grip.

The patrol motor cycle had a siren. It sounded now in warning response to the commotion going on by the far gate. Dave and the others ran off. Suzie's eyes flicked towards the old woman.

'Gotta go,' she said, thrusting the bag into her arms.

She ran off in the opposite direction. Towards the lake. Over the footbridge where the motor cycle couldn't follow. Through a gap in the fence. Out onto the road. She stopped, struggling to get her breath back. Had the others seen her run? Had they known she wouldn't hang around to play the hero? To name names. No Saint Suzie. Not today.

She was back in the house by ten fifteen. Early by her standards. Eric and Mel, who were creatures of habit, would be in the lounge watching the news. No need to disturb them. To answer questions about bruises and who she'd been hanging around with. To hear another lecture about her friends being trouble. Well, maybe they were but they were the only sort of friends she had. Or, maybe, didn't have any more.

She was half right about the Johnsons. They were in the lounge. The news was on. But they weren't watching.

95

They were examining some papers. Official looking papers which made Suzie change her plans. This could be news about Bessie.

The papers quickly disappeared into Mel's handbag as Suzie approached.

'What's so secret then?' said Suzie.

'Never mind that,' said Eric, leaping up. 'What the heck...'

'Fell off a wall.'

'You sure?'

''Course I'm bloody sure.'

'Let Mel bathe...'

'I'm all right. Stop fussin'. It's nowt. So what were them papers then?'

'Background on Pete's adoptive family,' said Mel. 'You know what it's like. These things have to be kept confidential.'

'Sure,' said Suzie, flopping onto the settee.

She tried to be patient as they probed and questioned about the wall. Where was it? How high was it? Who was she with? Had she blacked out at all? Did she have a headache? She answered but, for the first ten minutes, barely knew what she said. Vaguely hoped she was telling the right lies.

Her mind, which had been so full of Dave and the park when she came in, was now dominated by a single thought. Why had Mel lied to her? It wasn't like Mel to lie. But lie she had. Those papers weren't about Pete or his new adoptive family. They were about Anne Lister. Bessie's daughter. She had seen the name quite clearly on the top.

Suzie knew they didn't believe her about the wall. She didn't really care. She waited until they had given up and then changed the subject. Telling them about her day, about Justin and Mr Clarke and Matron's comments.

'And, by the way,' she said, as casually as she could. 'Has Sherlock Shaw come up with anythin' on Bessie's daughter yet? It'd be great if I could give Bessie a bit of news before I left.'

'Doesn't seem likely, Suzie,' said Mel, with barely a blush. 'He hasn't come up with anything new.'

Suzie went to bed with no intention of sleeping. At least you could say one thing about Eric and Mel. They were predictable. At precisely eleven thirty, she heard them come upstairs. Mel would leave her handbag on the chest of drawers by their bedroom window. She would read for half an hour.

Suzie waited. Half past twelve and they would be asleep. Another half hour to be really sure. It was easy enough. She'd done it before. When she was short of money. Mel's purse. Eric's jacket pocket. Not too much at a time. A pound or so here and there. Not enough for them to notice. Or, if they ever had, they hadn't mentioned it. Certainly they had never woken up. No reason why they should tonight.

Even so, Suzie was particularly careful. Creeping in, barefoot, reassured by the sound of Eric's snoring, she edged towards the chest of drawers, unzipped the bag and slowly removed the papers. She resisted the urge to turn and run, instead, moving calmly all the way back to her room.

She didn't use the lamp, in case one of the little ones noticed on their way to the toilet and stuck their snotty little nose in. She hunched over the papers by torchlight which did nothing to improve her hesitant reading.

Sherlock had been busy. There was tons of information all closely typed. Background on the adoptive parents. The work they did. Where they had lived. Where they had moved to. What schools Anne Lister had attended. What college she had gone to. Who she had married.

Suzie stopped and re-read that bit. Shaking her head, dismissing as coincidence what she saw. It was a common enough name after all. Moving on. Mr Lister's death, seven years ago. Mrs Lister's death only six months later. Back to Anne. Where she had worked... Coincidence again, surely? Then the trail went cold. There had been another move. Sherlock was working on it. More information to follow.

Was that why Mel had been so sneaky? Didn't want to raise any hopes until they had all the facts. Or was it more than that? Had Mel and Eric seen what she had seen? The possibility? The strangest, craziest, possibility?

No. It couldn't be, Suzie thought, as she crept back up the landing, into the bedroom, carefully replacing the papers. And if it was? What then? Was it something you could tell Bessie?

Back in her own room, Suzie started to laugh. Her teachers always said she had no imagination. But she had. Trouble was, it only surfaced at night. In the dark.

It was the darkness that brought the ghosts just as it was the darkness that conjured up crazy ideas about Bessie's daughter. It would all look so different in the morning.

Chapter 12

'It's for you,' Mel said, handing over the phone.

Suzie, who was just leaving for work, reluctantly turned back. It could only be Dave. Not like him to be up so early. He must be panicking about last night. Didn't he trust her at all?

'Justin?' she said, as she heard a male voice that couldn't possibly belong to Dave.

'I don't know. I don't usually get a lunch break. Well, yes, I suppose so. Just for half an hour.'

'A lunch date!' said Eric, raising his eyebrows as Suzie replaced the receiver.

'Don't be stupid,' Suzie snapped. 'Justin wants to talk to me, that's all. About the Manor. He were a bit shocked when I showed him round the other day.'

'The unofficial tour,' said Eric.

'Yeah. He said he's got a few ideas he wants to show me.'

'Original,' grinned Eric.

'Will you stop bein' daft. It's nowt like that. Someone like Justin wouldn't be interested in no one like me, would they? Anyway he's even older than Dave. Don't suppose you'd moan on so much if it were Justin though, would you?'

'As long as he didn't get you involved in too many revolutions, no, I don't suppose I would. Seriously though, don't forget this is your last two days at the

Manor. You're not going to change anything in two days, Suzie. With or without Justin's help.'

The few ideas turned out to be several pages of detailed plans, which Justin spread across the table of the coffee bar.

'That's right,' said Suzie, almost knocking over her milk shake. 'It'd be better like that. Offices downstairs, Matron's office and staff room knocked through to make a decent residents' lounge. That's brill. An' then what I thought was, you could use some of the car park for a garden.'

Justin scribbled it onto his notes.

'Not much you can do about those bedrooms,' he said. 'Apart from improve the decor and lighting.'

'Shouldn't think there's much we can do about anything,' said Suzie. 'I mean, makin' plans is one thing...but how d'you expect anyone to take notice?'

'I'm going to start with a polite request,' said Justin. 'I've got a meeting with Dr Grenville, Mr Forest and Matron this afternoon at three o'clock. Mum and Dad are coming to put a bit of weight behind it. Then if that doesn't work, another petition. I've already spoken to a few friends and relatives. I reckon I can get enough support. If enough of us threaten to remove our old folks...'

'Makes a difference, don't it?' said Suzie almost to herself.

'What?'

'Knowin' the right things to do. How to go about stuff. Bein' you, rather than me.'

101

'Don't run yourself down,' said Justin. 'It was you who got it all started. Gran's been in there three years now and we never bothered. Never thought about what was happening. We knew she was getting worse but we just put it down to age and her condition. Never really questioned the drugs she was getting or whether there was any stimulus. Or what her day-to-day life was like. You see things clearer than most and what's more you care about them. That's why I wanted to talk to you. I want you to come to the meeting.'

'Nah. I'd only put my foot in it. You'd be better off on your own. Eric says...'

'Who's Eric?'

'My foster dad. I told you. I'm in care.'

'Oh, yes,' said Justin, lowering his head.

'You don't need to be embarrassed about it.'

'I'm not... well, yes I am, in a way. I mean how...'

'My mum died. Overdose. Accidental death they said. And I haven't ever had a dad. So that's it really. I'm with Mel 'n' Eric now. Longest I've bin anywhere.'

'All right, are they?' said Justin, looking at Suzie's bruised face.

That story about the wall, she'd spun him earlier, didn't ring true.

'More than all right, I suppose. Must be to put up with me.'

'You do it a lot, don't you?'

'What?'

'Run yourself down.'

'Listen... if you knew what I were like. If you knew

one half the things I've done, you'd know why.'

'You mean like taking flowers into the Manor. Sitting talking to Gran for hours on end? Helping Harry with his jigsaws. Mr Vin...'

'Leave it out,' said Suzie. 'It aren't nothin' that. Come on, I've got to get back.'

Justin walked with her back to the Manor. He said he was going to spend some time with his gran before the meeting. He was disappointed when Suzie refused his repeated requests to go.

A refusal Suzie started to regret as the afternoon passed. She found it hard to concentrate, knowing what was going on upstairs in Matron's office. Watching the minutes tick by. Hanging on after work had finished, waiting for news. At five o'clock she went to check with Jill in reception. The meeting was still going on.

At five thirty, she was summoned to Matron's office. It was empty except for Matron herself.

'Sit down.'

Suzie sat.

'Well, I hope you're satisfied now.'

'I dunno,' said Suzie. 'Tell me what you're on about an' I'll let you know.'

'Don't play the innocent with me,' said Matron. 'It might have been Justin and his parents sitting here making demands but I know where they sprang from.'

'I showed Justin what went on, that's all.'

'There's no need to be so defensive,' said Matron. 'I'm not getting at you. I can't say I approve of your methods or your attitude but they're effective. I can't count the times I've pleaded for extra staff, re-decoration, a garden out front. Only to be told it's too expensive. It can't be done. Now they're talking about a complete restructure. Putting the residents' lounge upstairs...'

'Blimey! They agreed to that!'

'They agreed to everything,' said Matron. 'Mr Forest kicked off by saying he hadn't a penny to spare, as usual. Dr Grenville insisted that the residents were in comparatively good health. But once your friend Justin had pointed out how many people were prepared to withdraw their relatives, if nothing was done, they soon changed their minds. All a matter of economics really.'

'An' what about you? What d'you think? About your office bein' put in the basement an' stuff.'

'It's not going to affect me. I'm resigning.'

''Cos of that?'

'In a way. I wanted to see a few changes before I left and now they've all come at once, I can leave with a clear conscience. I suppose I've got you to thank for that. Which leads me to the other reason I sent for you. Your report.'

'Oh, that.'

'Yes that. Oh, for heaven's sake can't you stop being so sullen?' Matron snapped.

'It's the way I'm made.'

'Forgive me if I beg to differ,' said Matron. 'But I don't think there's anything wrong with the way you're made. It's what you choose to do to yourself, the way you choose to act, which causes the problems. Look at you! You're attractive, healthy…'

'Thick.'

'Maybe not clever in the accepted sense, but you're smart enough and you've got a real talent with the old people, which is what I've put in my report. But you'll never use it, will you? You'll slouch through life feeling sorry for yourself, telling yourself you can't do it. Brooding about whatever it is you brood about. Getting angry. Blaming the world for your problems.'

'I don't have to listen to this,' snapped Suzie.

'No you don't. I never really expected you to. But let me give you some advice for free. It's no good living your life in the past. Wondering what might have happened if. You have to accept what you are, where you are, and get on with life.'

'Oh, sure. That's right easy, that is. What do you know about it?'

'Perhaps more than you think,' said Matron. 'When I was your age, my parents told me I was adopted. I went around with a chip on my shoulder about it for years. Blaming them for not telling me earlier. Blaming them for adopting me at all. Wondering what was so awful about me that my birth parents didn't want me. Making life hell for everyone around me. Until, eventually, when I'd convinced myself that I was completely dull and worthless, I had a breakdown. Only when my parents had helped me pick up the pieces, did I start to see things differently. I…'

Suzie had stopped listening after the first sentence. She stared at Matron, trying to slot the pieces into place.

Toying with the one fragment which refused to fit.

'Marie,' she said.

Matron stopped speaking, astonished both by the interruption and by the use of her first name.

'Marie,' Suzie repeated. 'That is your name, isn't it? That's what your husband said.'

'Well, yes. That's what Jack calls me. It's my middle name actually. But it was a bit confusing with his sister and mother being called Anne.'

'So your name's Anne?'

'Yes but I don't see . . .'

'And you're adopted?'

Matron nodded.

'An' did you ever try to trace your birth parents?'

'No. That's what I meant about living in the past. Fretting about what might have been. Why should I go delving around, finding out things I probably don't want to know? They didn't want me. Couldn't keep me. Whatever. I nearly drove myself mad worrying about it once. Then after the breakdown, I said to myself, what's the point? You've had a good life. You've got parents who love you. Leave well alone.'

'So you wouldn't ever want to know?'

'No. Definitely not! Are you all right? You look a bit pale and that bruise . . . how did . . .'

'Yeah. I mean no. Fell off a wall. Bit of a headache. Can I go now?'

Suzie stood outside Matron's office trying to get her thoughts together. Bessie. Matron. Matron. Bessie. The baby who became Anne-Marie Lister, who became Mrs

106

Clarke, who ended up in charge of the home where her own mother was a resident without even knowing it. Crazy! No wonder Mel had tried to hide those papers! What a mess! And what was she supposed to do now? Tell Bessie? Matron? Both? Neither? Talk to Mel? Confess she'd been rooting around in her handbag?

'Great news, isn't it?'

'What?' she said, as Justin appeared apparently from nowhere.

'Thought I'd wait. Mum and Dad want you to come and have dinner with us tonight. A sort of celebration.'

'Dinner.'

'You know. Food. Eating. I want to show you the revised plans. They've agreed to . . . '

Justin rambled on as they walked, before realising that Suzie wasn't listening.

'Suzie?'

'Sorry. I was thinking. I've got a bit of a problem.'

'I think I've just seen him.'

'Him?'

Almost without Suzie noticing, they had left the Manor and were nearly at the end of the track. Where the track met the main road, Dave was waiting, waving at them.

'You know him?' Justin asked, as Dave raised his hand again.

'He's a friend.'

Why had she said that? Why not admit it? Dave was her boyfriend. Ex-boyfriend, whatever.

He ambled towards them, blocking their path.

107

'Who's this?' he said, without bothering with pleasantries.

'Justin,' said Suzie. 'He's bin visitin' his gran.'

'Fine,' said Dave. 'Now he can...'

Justin looked at Suzie, wincing at Dave's words. At the bruises on her cheek which he'd half thought the foster parents had done.

'What d'you want, Dave?' said Suzie, wearily.

'I wanna talk ter yer. About the other night.'

'Not now. I'm shattered. I can't be doing with...'

'Yeah. Now,' Dave insisted. 'So get rid of 'im before he finds out what sorta person's bin lookin' after 'is granny.'

'I know what sort of person she is, actually.'

'Oh do yer, actually,' Dave sneered.

'Listen,' said Suzie. 'I didn't say nowt, the other night. Not to nobody. An' I won't neither. So you can stop hasslin' me about it. Okay?'

'I'm not hasslin'. I just wanna talk ter yer. Come on, Suze. Yer don't wanna hang about with that jerk. Let's go round my house. I'm tryin ter make up.'

His smile lit up his face, making him look younger, not so tough. Reminding Suzie of how she felt. Of how she'd wanted him all those months he'd been going out with Dina. He was her type. The sort of bloke she'd been brought up with. The kind that used to come and see her mum.

She looked at him, feeling the force of the attraction almost pulling her towards him. She didn't want to finish with him, did she? She'd just spent every penny of her money, and more borrowed from Mel, on a helmet to go with the motor bike his dad was getting him for his birthday. He'd promised to take her out on it in the holidays. They'd planned...

'Well,' said Dave. 'You comin' or not?'

Suzie looked at Justin. Thought of Lily, Bessie, the old woman in the park.

'No,' she said, turning away. 'No I'm not.'

Chapter 13

Suzie burst into tears as Dave turned and walked away. Tears of relief more than regret. But Justin didn't know that. Didn't know that Dave, in a different mood, could have turned very nasty.

'I'm sorry,' Justin said, putting his arms round Suzie.

The embrace was comforting, warm, brotherly rather than amorous but Suzie pulled away, anyway.

'It don't matter. I knew it were over, the other night... I don't suppose you ride a motor bike, do you?'

'No, why?'

'Nothin'.'

'I borrow Dad's car when I need to. Shall I pick you up tonight?'

'What?'

'Dinner...'

'No. I aren't coming.'

'Because of him?'

'No.'

'Why then?'

'For someone who's supposed to be clever you're pretty dumb, aren't you? Your parents'd 'ave a fit, if they met me! I wouldn't know how to act, what to say or nothin'.'

'It's not some sort of test!' said Justin. 'Can't you just relax? Be yourself.'

'No. No I can't,' said Suzie.

110

That was the trouble, Suzie thought, as she sprawled on the lounge floor, pretending to watch television. People like Justin made it sound so easy. Be yourself. But who was she supposed to be? Two weeks ago it had all seemed so obvious. And now, here she was, campaigning for a bunch of geriatrics and being invited to dinner by someone who went to Oxford University.

Eric asked her why she was laughing.

'I were thinking.'

'Things are looking up.'

She threw a cushion at him.

'I've got somethin' to ask you,' she said, changing the tone in an instant. 'Why didn't you tell me?'

'About?'

'About Bessie.'

'How did you . . . '

Mel put down the school shirt she was mending and shook her head at Eric. No point asking how Suzie knew.

'I'm sorry,' said Mel. 'It was a bit delicate. We wanted to think about it first. Make sure.'

'And have you?'

'Yes.'

'So have I.'

'Suzie! You haven't told . . . '

'What d'you take me for? No, don't answer that. But I 'ad a lecture from Matron today. She let on she were adopted. Said she didn't want to know nowt about her birth parents . . . '

'A lot of people don't,' said Eric. 'The question is, do we respect those wishes or do we have an obligation to

111

your friend, Bessie?'

'A what?'

'Obligation. A duty to tell her what we've found.'

'I 'ad an idea about that,' said Suzie. 'Oh, an' by the way, I've stopped seeing Dave.'

Mel, who was used to Suzie's butterfly mind, took in the information, stored it for a later date and went back to Bessie.

'What sort of idea?'

'I thought we could just tell 'er what she wanted to know all along. That her daughter was alive and okay an' everythin'.'

'Wouldn't that make things worse?' said Eric. 'Wouldn't she want to know more? And what if she started talking about it? What if Matron somehow caught on? Oh, I don't know…'

'Maybe we should wait,' said Suzie. 'Matron says she's retirin' soon. Maybe we could tell Bessie once she's gone. Oh, God, I wish I'd never started any of this. I wish I'd never set foot in the bloody place.'

It wasn't true, of course. Setting foot in the Manor was the best thing that had happened to her in years. And now it was over. Almost over. Friday. Her last day. Barely an hour left. She set out the tea things in the residents' lounge, trying to smile, trying to talk. At least things were looking up. All the old people looked smart today. Very smart. And Trish had said that the first phase of the re-structuring programme would start in a fortnight.

There had been one disappointment earlier in the day. She'd asked Mr Vincent if he'd managed to do the cartoon of her which she'd asked for.

'Sorry, love,' he'd said. 'I tried but my shakes came on bad and...'

'That's okay,' Suzie had said hurriedly. 'I understand.'

And then there was Bessie. She hadn't really liked lying to Bessie. Telling the story she'd finally agreed with Mel and Eric.

'We found out about the family,' she'd said. 'They were right nice people. I'm sure your daughter would have been happy with them. She were clever too. Went to a grammar school. But then they moved and we 'aven't bin able to trace 'em.'

Bessie had asked questions, of course, and seemed vaguely satisfied with the answers, smiling and nodding to herself, like poor Edward Tyler used to do.

Clearly it had disturbed her. Half truths, Suzie decided, were probably the worst kind. Best to know or not know. But she had promised Mel, so there it was. Done.

'Suzie, I need some help in the office,' Jill called.

'But I'm...'

'Trish'll do tea.'

Suzie shrugged and followed. No point arguing; trying to explain that she wanted to spend her limited time with the residents, not clearing out cupboards in the office. Besides, Mrs Dolby would be here soon. Doing her final check.

In the event, it was even more stupid than clearing out

cupboards. Jill only wanted her to water the plants, most of which were swimming around in their pots anyway.

'There's only one needs doing.'

'Oh, right ... well check the ...'

'Couldn't I go ...'

'No.'

She'd said it so firmly that Suzie half expected to be there for the night doing jobs that clearly didn't need doing. Ten minutes later the phone rang and Jill shoved a piece of paper into her hand.

'Take that to Trish, down in the lounge, will you?'

Another stupid job. The note was asking about the following week's menu, something Jill would normally check by phone. What was going on?

Suzie knew as soon as she walked through the door. It all came together. Why the residents were so well dressed. Why she'd been called away to the office. This was a party! A farewell party. For her. Even so, it took a while to sink in. The cake that Pat had made. The enormous card, propped up behind it. The people. Not only staff and residents but Justin and Mrs Dolby too.

She had to blink to force back the tears. She'd look a right prat if she cried. Trish came forward, pushing a rectangular present into her hand.

'Thanks I ...'

'Don't thank me,' said Trish. 'I was going to get you a card but it was the residents who insisted on all this. Mr Vincent ...'

She didn't have to continue. It was obvious, as Suzie unwrapped the present, what Mr Vincent's contribution

114

had been. He'd done what she'd asked... and more. A large cartoon with Suzie in the centre, surrounded by the residents, balancing placards on their wheelchairs, signing petitions and shaking their walking sticks. He'd called it the Wheelchair Revolution.

Suddenly what people thought barely mattered any more. Suzie started to cry.

'I'm all right,' she managed to stutter, as Justin hurried over. 'I just don't want to leave, that's all.'

'Why do it then?' said Bessie. 'You don't have to.'

''Course I do, Bess,' said Suzie, kneeling down and clutching her hand. 'I'm only fourteen you know. I don't even finish school for another year or so.'

'There's weekends.'

'What?'

'You could come at the weekend, sometimes. Just to see us. Or to help out. As a sort of Saturday job.'

'That's right,' said Lily. 'Our Justin used to help out in a newsagent's at weekends.'

'I don't know,' said Matron.

'And why not?' said Mr Vincent.

'It's a bit unusual... I don't know what Dr Grenville and Mr Forest will say.'

'That's right,' said Bessie. 'Use them as your excuse. You always do.'

'That's hardly fair...'

'Fair!' said Bessie. 'You can talk about fair after everything that's gone on here? You were the one who almost dropped Suzie at the end of the first week. I tell you, she's done more...'

'Don't,' said Suzie, quietly. 'Please don't.'

'Don't what?' said Bessie.

'Argue. About me. I aren't worth it. You might say somatt you'd regret if you ever found out...'

'I've already found out. And it doesn't make matters any different.'

'But you can't have,' Suzie exclaimed. 'You can't have worked it out from what I told you.'

'Not what you told me no...'

'Then how? Nobody else here knew we were looking, let alone about Sherlock's papers. It took me long enough to cotton on. What with Matron calling herself Marie instead of Anne and...'

Suzie stopped mid sentence. Something was wrong. Bessie's eyes didn't register anything of course but the rest of her body did. She was suddenly tense. Agitated. As if this were a shock... as if she hadn't known at all.

'What are you talking about?' Bessie asked, while everyone else looked totally bemused.

'You said you'd found out. You said you knew who your daugh... didn't you?'

'I was talking about you, dear,' said Bessie, quietly. 'I've been finding out about you. From Justin and Mrs Dolby. About your background and the bother you've been in. And it doesn't make any difference to me. You're still my lovely Suzie. But we've been talking at cross purposes, haven't we? You've found out something else, haven't you? Something you haven't told me.'

Suzie nodded her head. Tried to speak when she

116

realised Bessie couldn't see her acknowledgement. Couldn't speak.

'Something Matron knows...' Bessie prompted.

'Me!' said Matron. 'I'm the last person to know anything around here these days. Why should I know anything? Perhaps you could enlighten us, Suzie.'

'I'm sorry,' said Suzie, ignoring everyone but Bessie. 'I knew I'd make a muck of it. Me and my big mouth. An' now I'll have to tell you everythin'. But not now. Not here.'

'It's her,' said Bessie, starting to laugh. 'It's Matron, isn't it? That's what you've found out. Matron's my daughter.'

'Trish, get Bessie's pills,' said Matron, as Bessie's laughter increased. 'She's rambling. She's got over-excited. I knew what would happen if...'

'She don't need pills,' said Suzie. 'An' she's not ramblin'. She's right. It's true. She 'ad a kid that was adopted. She keeps the picture in her purse. Me an' Mel 'ave bin checking for 'er. We were almost sure, then the other day when you said you were adopted...'

It was like a film, Suzie thought. Suddenly everybody was talking and then, equally suddenly, it fell quiet again. Everyone looking at everyone else. Expecting reactions, which came, almost in slow motion. Bessie's laughter turning to tears. Lily Smith muttering, 'Oh my goodness,' over and over again. And the full bulk of Matron crashing to the floor in a dead faint.

Chapter 14

Suzie stood by the classroom window, gazing out onto the playground, waiting for the others to turn up.

'Are you still helping at the Manor?' Mrs Dolby asked.

'Yeah. I spent most of the summer holiday there an' I still go most weekends.'

'Even now Bessie's gone?'

Suzie nodded.

'Bessie were special. But then, I love Elsie and Lily and the others too.'

She hadn't used the word lightly. It was love, of a kind. When someone needed you. She supposed it was the sort of love people felt for their babies. Ugly, screaming things to an outsider but so dependent. So vulnerable. Made you realise how hard it would have been for someone like Bessie...

'And besides,' she said, swinging round to face Mrs Dolby, 'Matron says I can go round and visit any time I like.'

'It was strange the way that turned out,' Mrs Dolby said.

It had certainly been strange at first. Trish reviving Matron. Calling her husband and Dr Grenville. Everyone else trying to calm the residents. Helping Bessie come to terms with the shock.

But, within a few days, she had done more than come

to terms with it. And so had Matron. They spent hours cloistered together, talking, filling in the gaps in their lives that had spanned fifty years.

Bessie's grand-daughter and great-grandchildren came to visit. Then, when Matron had worked her notice, it had seemed only natural to invite Bessie to live with them.

'Mmmm,' said Suzie, aware she was responding very slowly to Mrs Dolby's comments. 'I were dead relieved, that it turned out okay. An' it's nice for Bessie. I mean she don't need a load of medical treatment or nothing. There's no real reason for her to be in one of them homes. No reason for the likes of Lily Smith neither except their families don't want 'em. You know what I think?'

'No,' said Mrs Dolby, who was still struggling to come to terms with the fact that Suzie had taken up thinking at all.

'I think they should have foster homes for old folks, like they do for kids. I mean it's much better an' I should know. I always got on better in foster homes than I did in them big kids' homes. Some are better than others, of course. Mel 'n' Eric'd be great at it.'

'Perhaps you could make that the subject of your next piece of work, Suzie. Look at the factors for and against. Examine how it might be done. Whether you think enough people would come forward to ... er ... foster. It's certainly an original idea.'

'I told Justin about it and he agreed with me.'

'You still see him, do you?' said Mrs Dolby, trying to eliminate all traces of surprise from her voice.

119

'Not now. He's back at university. But he writes. An' I saw 'im a lot in the summer. He's okay is Justin. Dead brainy but he aren't a snob. He never laughs at me or nothing.'

'Why should he?'

'You know, the way I talk an' stuff.'

Mrs Dolby looked at Suzie, now perched on the edge of one of the desks. Although her grammar hadn't actually improved, she had started to sound different this term. Less confrontational. And she certainly looked different. Only one set of studs, today. Wearing some of the uniform. Make-up still there but more discreet.

Mrs Dolby had thought it had something to do with the Manor. Now she was inclined to think it might be Justin's influence. Funny friendship that was!

Unbeknown to Mrs Dolby, Mel and Eric had said something very similar over the holiday.

'That's all we are, you know,' Suzie had snapped. 'Friends. His parents would go ballistic if they thought it were anythin' else. They're like you were about Dave. Act like there's a nasty smell when I'm around. But Justin's okay. And, I mean if I didn't see Justin, I wouldn't be goin' out at all, would I? Not now Gemma's taken up with Dave. I can't hang around with that lot no more, can I? Don't know what I'm supposed to do when term starts.'

It had been hard at first. Gemma had left but Lisa was still around, spreading rumours, talking behind Suzie's back, turning the old crowd against her. There'd been some bother at the start of the second week when Suzie

120

had got fed up with it and thrown a chair at Lisa during a French lesson.

Suzie had been suspended and Mel and Eric called in to see the Head. Together with Mrs Dolby, they'd pleaded for Suzie to be allowed to stay. In the end, she'd changed classes and signed a contract about her behaviour.

Mel and Eric had talked about another sort of contract too. They'd said they wanted to adopt her.

'Nah,' she'd said after giving it some thought. 'It'd be stupid, wouldn't it? You wouldn't get paid nowt if I were adopted, like you do for fostering. An' it'd be too sort of final, wouldn't it? If I wanted to go or if you wanted rid of me. So I reckon we should leave things as they are. I mean I sorta think of you as my mum an' dad now... not that I'd ever forget my real mum.'

Mel had nodded, smiled, yet looked close to tears, making Suzie wonder whether she'd said the right thing.

Probably. Adoption was a big step. Like marriage. Too much of a commitment. But it was nice of them and she'd promised herself she'd try not to cause them too much hassle.

She hadn't done badly since then, she thought, turning round as some of the others drifted into the classroom. One or two rows about staying out late, swearing and making a mess around the house... but all families had them, didn't they? And they weren't too keen on Phil, her new boyfriend. Said he was as bad as Dave. But then you had to be realistic, didn't you? Now Justin was back with the posh girls at Oxford, he'd probably stop writing to her. Still, on the quiet, it was him she thought about.

She shrugged and went and sat next to Laura, as she always did now.

Mrs Dolby smiled as she handed out paper. Laura wasn't what you'd call bright but she was pleasant enough. Very quiet and placid. A good friend for Suzie. Like stabling a donkey with a highly strung racehorse to calm it down.

This was Mrs Dolby's special group, the one that met at lunchtime, where kids who needed a bit of extra help could come and do homework or practise basic skills. Today they were doing some writing.

The door opened, just as the group had settled.

'I wondered if I could give this to Laura,' Mr Pugh said. 'It's a leaflet about careers in the Hotel Industry.'

Mrs Dolby nodded, curtly, as Mr Pugh deposited the leaflet and stood hovering over the desk.

'That looks interesting, Suzie,' he said. 'Your writing's come on a bit, hasn't it?'

He tried to resist the temptation to smirk, as he looked at Mrs Dolby.

'Have you read that information I gave you about N.V.Q.s?'

'Yeah,' said Suzie. 'Looks all right that. You know you can do 'em while you're workin', if you can get a placement somewhere. An' Trish is sure the Manor'll take me on, specially if I keep goin' at weekends and stuff. It's tons better now except that Mr Forest's dead grumpy about all the money he's had to spend.'

'I think Suzie ought to get on, now,' said Mrs Dolby, almost pushing her colleague out of the door.

She, as much as anyone, was delighted by Suzie's improved attitude, but there was no way she was having Bryan Pugh hanging around gloating and saying I told you!

She stared down at the playground, at Lisa and her friends disappearing behind the gym for a smoke. Nothing much ever changed for most of these kids. But occasionally...

'Is this all right, Miss?'

She took Suzie's paper and looked at the side of almost legible writing. Okay, so it wasn't brilliant but it was a start.

'The problim of caring for old peepel.'

'I'll finish it at home,' said Suzie. 'I've bin collectin' articles out of the newspapers. Justin started me off during the holidays. You'd be amazed at the abuse that goes on in some of them places. Makes the Manor look like a blood... sorry, Miss, flippin' paradise. I'll sort 'em out an' do it like a kind of project. Then I could use it for part of my assessment, couldn't I? And then I thought...'

There it was again. The impossible. Suzie Lawrence. Thinking. Mrs Dolby stopped looking down and looked skyward instead... just to see if there were any pigs flying over the playground.